A Candlelight Ecstasy Romance®

"SPARKS FLY EVERY TIME WE SEE EACH OTHER," JESSICA SAID IN A HUSKY VOICE.

"I wonder why?" Grant murmured, reaching out to take her shoulders in his hands.

"I provoke you?" she whispered.

"You are provocative," he agreed.

"I'm building a pool you don't want?"

"I want the builder, not the pool," he corrected.

"I smashed your car?"

"And my equilibrium."

"You should hate me."

"I should hate what you're doing to me." The sweet, coaxing tip of his tongue traced the bow of her lower lip.

"What am I doing to you?" Jessica mouthed against his lips in a breathy whisper.

"This," he replied, pulling her even closer. "Pushing me to the brink of my self-control."

CANDLELIGHT ECSTASY CLASSIC ROMANCES

CANDLELIGHT ECSTASY ROMANCES®

REBEL
LOVE

Anna Hudson

A CANDLELIGHT ECSTASY ROMANCE®

Published by
Dell Publishing Co., Inc.
1 Dag Hammarskjold Plaza
New York, New York 10017

ISBN: 0-440-17413-9

Printed in the United States of America

December 1986

10 9 8 7 6 5 4 3 2 1

WFH

*Dedicated to Kenneth Kaye for his expertise,
his honesty, and his forbearance.*

To Our Readers:

We have been delighted with your enthusiastic response to Candlelight Ecstasy Romances®, and we thank you for the interest you have shown in this exciting series.

In the upcoming months we will continue to present the distinctive sensuous love stories you have come to expect only from Ecstasy. We look forward to bringing you many more books from your favorite authors and also the very finest work from new authors of contemporary romantic fiction.

As always, we are striving to present the unique, absorbing love stories that you enjoy most—books that are more than ordinary romance. Your suggestions and comments are always welcome. Please write to us at the address below.

Sincerely,

The Editors
Candlelight Romances
1 Dag Hammarskjold Plaza
New York, New York 10017

CHAPTER ONE

"What the devil do you think you're doing?" Grant McDougal demanded of the petite blonde who was pounding small flagged stakes into the sandy soil.

The booming voice with its northern twang startled Jessica. The hammer she'd been using slipped from her grasp. "Staking the excavation site," she answered sharply.

"Not in this yard!"

Jessica Hayes struggled to keep herself from picking up the hammer and tossing it behind her in the direction of the voice. This hadn't been a gold-star day in the history of Plantation Pools. In fact, complications installing a pool filter had drained her patience, delayed her schedule, and forced her to work long past her regular hours.

Daylight had dwindled hours ago, and so had her patience. What she needed was a frosty mint julep and a soft easy chair. What she didn't need was a nosy neighbor interfering with the construction of this pool.

Her bones aching, she stood up, keeping her back to the belligerent intruder. She stretched and blinked her eyes against the direct glare of the backyard floodlight. Despite the protest her muscles made, her grayish-blue eyes twinkled with mischief.

"According to our calculations, they should be located somewhere within the radius of these flags."

"They? Precisely what are *they?*"

Jessica grinned, noting the appreciable drop in the volume of his voice. His tone had changed, too. Curiosity was now blended with irritation. She delayed answering by stooping to pick up the hammer and hooking it into the loop of her gray jumpsuit. Her mind raced for a suitably impressive reply as she straightened, her back still to him.

Dinosaur bones? She swiftly discarded that idea. To her recollection none had been uncovered in South Carolina. *Confederate cannons?* Appropriate, but trite. A breath of salty air blowing in off the Charleston harbor gave her the clue she needed. She stuck her tongue in her cheek, rolled it, then gravely answered, "Chief Wampum's pyramid."

She was tempted to glance over her shoulder to see his reaction, but she knew she'd lose her composure and laugh, spoiling her windy tale. If he believed her, perhaps he wouldn't interfere until the pool equipment arrived. Besides, she didn't want him to see the Plantation Pools logo on the front of her uniform. She could feel his eyes boring a hole between her shoulder blades deep enough for a diving tank.

"Do you have a permit?"

"Certainly." She heard his heavy footsteps behind her. She stepped into a dark shadow cast by a live oak that was dripping with Spanish moss. Strategically, now she had the advantage: She could see him, but her neutral clothing and fair coloring blended into the darkness. Her eyes narrowed as she assessed the intruder. *Big* and *brawny* were her first thoughts. Begrudgingly, she added *handsome*. But not in the classic, pretty-boy way that usually appealed to her. His strong features appeared to have been chiseled from sleek teak. Only a slight crook in his otherwise-straight nose marred his perfection. Wide-set, clear blue eyes were shooting silvery glints in her direction.

The tall man angrily facing her wasn't intrigued the way she'd hoped he would be. Her mind raced for facts to substantiate her outlandish claim. "Chief Wampum's pyramid is the missing link between American history and Egypt. Don't you know who he was?"

The stranger made a disparaging noise that sounded like a curse. "Chief Wampum, my foot!"

"Your foot may be right at the peak of the pyramid." Jessica quickly pounded a stake to mark the spot while mentally weaving the fib further. She pressed her forefinger over her middle finger as she spun an intricate white lie that spanned two civilizations. "Our calculations may be a bit off, but you can't expect Egyptian archaeologists to be precise. Goodness, they don't even live on this continent, much less here in Charleston. They believe the great Indian chief, whose ancestors were Egyptian, brought his tribe south during the Great Snowstorm of 1822 in New York State. We have proof that he made lots of wampum by selling shrimp to the Americans. In fact, he paid for indentured servants to build a monument to his forefathers—a pyramid. And we think the peak of the pyramid is"—she gestured toward the flags— "right about here!"

For a few seconds, there was absolute, total silence. Then his voice raised: *"Rose!"*

11

Jessica recognized the first name of the elderly woman who'd signed the contract to build the pool. She surmised that this stranger with the sonic-boom voice might have influence with her employer.

Should she come clean? Laugh off her little fib as a joke? Or should she stick to her guns? Although she'd only met with Rose McDougal briefly on three occasions, Jessica felt certain that the spritely lady would play along with her. After all, Mrs. McDougal had been adamant about getting the pool built as quickly as possible. But on the other hand, she didn't want to start a feud between Rose McDougal and her neighbor.

Jessica sank further into the canopy of darkness. Her foot stumbled over a gnarled root as her shoulders touched the coarse bark of the tree. Further retreat wasn't possible. She had to attack or surrender.

"Calling Mrs. McDougal isn't necessary. Actually, I'm staking out Mrs. McDougal's swimming pool."

When she saw the scowl on his rugged face deepen, Jessica Hayes fingered the five-pound hammer for protection. The truth suited him less than the fib had. She should have stuck to the Chief Wampum pyramid story. She'd spoiled a perfectly good joke by ruining the punch line. If killing looks meant anything, *she* was about to be buried now, without any marker. With a show of mock bravery, she smiled in a friendly manner and extended her hand. "Jessica Hayes, Plantation Pools. We design. We install. We attend the first pool party."

"You may have designs on Rose McDougal's pocketbook, but you aren't about to install a pool in this yard, much less attend any social gatherings here. So if

you'll kindly hustle your little fanny out of this yard—
and stay out—I'd appreciate it," the stranger gritted
with menace.

Insulted at being ordered off the premises and at
being accused of trying to bilk an old lady, Jessica's
hand clenched around the hammer head. For a single
impetuous moment, she wished she could indulge in a
little head-to-head combat with this rude Yankee; her
hammer head versus his skull would even out the difference in their heights. Her quick temper cooled to
Arctic iciness. A businesswoman didn't indulge in vio-
lent whims, regardless of how deserving the object of
those whims might be of it.

"Who are you to order me from the premises?"

"The man with the title to this house. Grant
McDougal."

"I have a contract with the *lady* who owns this
house. If you'll kindly step aside, I'll get it from the
briefcase in my truck."

Grant turned sideways and extended his hand toward the turquoise blue pickup truck in the McDougal's driveway.

As Jessica briskly walked past him, she noticed the
clean smell of Ivory soap. She regretted not having
stopped by her house long enough to change clothes
and wash the residue of Gunite mix from her face and
hair. Grant McDougal's height and breadth were in-
timidating, and the contrast between his cleanliness
and her concrete-encrusted clothing set her feminine
teeth on edge.

She opened the cab door and pulled a brown leather
briefcase out onto the driver's seat. She hated being at
a disadvantage with any man, but for some unknown

reason, she particularly hated having Grant McDougal intimidate her. She unsnapped the briefcase with a vengeance and pulled the folder labeled MCDOUGAL from the small stack of manila files containing current Plantation Pools contracts.

Handing him the McDougal folder, she summarily dismissed his immaculate appearance. Although the muscles beneath his navy blue cotton polo shirt denied the possibility, Jessica pegged him as a pencil pusher, a man who didn't know the first thing about the construction business.

"A performance clause and a thirty-day completion date? At least mother had sense enough not to let a pool builder take the down payment and leave her with a hole in the backyard for months on end," he commented, thinking aloud.

Jessica bristled. Had Grant seen the Plantation Pools logo on the truck and connected it with the past reputation of her company? In grim silence she cursed Nicky Walton, the man she'd divorced three years ago. Nicky had fled Charleston with company money in his pocket, leaving seven gaping holes in the backyards of various unhappy customers. How long would it take to rebuild the company's reputation after that fiasco? She'd retained her maiden name but not the pristine reputation associated with it.

She was angry with herself, with Nicky, and particularly with this arrogant man. She had picked up on the faint trace of New England accent in Grant McDougal's voice. With a thicker-than-cream southern drawl, she drew an imaginary Mason-Dixon Line between them by retorting, "Mr. McDougal, I believe history will verify that northern carpetbaggers invaded

14

the South to rape the countryside of its wealth, not the other way around. Why don't you return to your polluted industrial city up north and leave the South in the capable hands of us southern ladies?"

"Ladies? You're including yourself in that classification?" His blue eyes swept over her untidy hair and soiled jumpsuit as if to emphasize her lack of qualifications for that category. Jessica Hayes was a century away from corsets, hoop skirts, and parasols, and yet she had the audacity to fling the Confederate flag in his face!

Forcing her lips to remain in a slight upward curve, speaking at the same soft, slow level, she answered, "Being a lady is a state of mind, not an avocation. Scarlett O'Hara didn't mind getting her hands dirty when the necessity arose."

Poker-faced, Grant appeared to ignore the velvet-coated-steel jibe as he flipped to the final page of the contract. "My Civil War history is a bit rusty, but I seem to recall that the name for southerners who did business with the invaders was *scalawag.*"

His curved finger rubbed over his smoothly shaven chin as he waited for Jessica's reaction. He glanced upward in time to catch her flicking her tongue nervously across the enticing bow of her bottom lip. Surprised by his own immediate reaction to the beckoning gloss of moisture that her tongue left behind, he added, "You aren't a copperhead by chance, are you?"

"A northern sympathizer? Not likely. My name is on the active members' list of the United Daughters of the Confederacy."

"Too bad." He envisioned speculatively what might lie beneath her grimy exterior and the jumpsuit that

15

accented her womanly curves. Then he realized he'd taken his frustration at being unable to control his mother's impetuosity out on Jennifer. One side of his mouth slanted into a lopsided smile. "I've had a hard day. I could use a bit of sympathy."

Jennifer showed her contempt for the all-too-familiar leer on his face by plucking the contract from his hand. "Sympathizers were shot. I'm expecting to live to the ripe old age of a hundred."

"Trespassers are also shot, Ms. Hayes."

As she returned the contract to her briefcase, Jessica inwardly shivered at the ice in his voice. "Exactly what is your objection to backyard pools?"

"They're dangerous."

"My understanding from your mother is that she's been in water therapy for her arthritis for months."

"Her therapy is conducted at the hospital under supervision. In case you hadn't noticed, she lives alone."

Mentally, Jessica stored that tidbit of information. "She intends to have friends over to swim. Therapy and social activity, I believe, are the words your mother chose. Far more enjoyable than tediously sitting in a hospital pool supervised by an attendant."

"But far less safe. Aside from my mother's safety, what about the neighborhood children?"

"An eight-foot decorative fence will surround the pool."

Grant snorted derisively. "A fence never stopped me when I was a kid."

"I'll bet it didn't," Jessica muttered, thinking he was probably born six feet tall and as agile as a panther.

16

When they heard Mrs. McDougal calling Jessica, both of them turned toward the back veranda.

"Coming," Jessica shouted. Automatically, she started to dismiss Grant by sticking her hand forward for a businesslike handshake. But then she remembered his first reaction and rubbed her hand down the side of her thigh. She nodded curtly in his direction. "Excuse me."

"Oh, no, Jessica Hayes, I'm coming with you. We're going to get this matter straightened out immediately."

Jessica grinned. "Something tells me my equipment will be arriving on schedule tomorrow morning."

"What makes you think my mother will defy my decision?"

"A signed contract"—her impish smile broadened—"and the slight hint of a Kentucky drawl in your mother's voice."

"Kentucky was a border state—neutral."

Leading the way, Jessica retorted over her shoulder, "One belle can recognize the refined tones of another belle."

Grant stopped at the bottom of the wooden steps to the house. Her melodious, soft laughter, which followed the taunt, sent a shiver of apprehension down his spine. He suspected that Jessica Hayes and Rose McDougal would have been worthy adversaries for General Sherman. Hell's bells, he could already taste the ashes of defeat, and the main skirmish hadn't even begun yet.

"Son, I didn't expect you to drop by this evening," Rose greeted him pleasantly. "I was just about to offer

Jessica some freshly squeezed lemonade. Will you join us?"

Bending down a foot, Grant kissed his mother's up-turned cheek. "Perhaps something a bit stronger?"

"Southern Comfort on the rocks?" Jessica mischievously suggested.

"Oh dear," Rose mumbled through the fingers covering her mouth. "He knows?"

"He knows," Jessica confirmed.

"Mother dear—" Grant began.

"Sounds like 'Mommie Dearest,' doesn't it, Jessica?" Rose's blue eyes twinkled with contained mirth as she watched Jessica bob her head up and down. "Not to worry, I promise that his bark is worse than his bite."

"Don't make any promises you can't keep." Grant motioned for Jessica and his mother to be seated in the green-cushioned white rattan chairs. "Sit down, please."

Rose called into the nearby kitchen, "Sara, would you be so kind as to bring three lemonades to the veranda? Add a jigger of Kentucky bourbon to one of them, please." Seating herself at a corner of the sofa, she raised her chin defiantly toward her son. "Now don't start ordering us around like little tin soldiers. I've decided I'm going to have a pool. And after talking to Jessica, I decided that Plantation Pools would be the builder."

Sitting down in the chair opposite Jessica, Grant stretched his legs out and crossed them at the ankle. His relaxed pose didn't fool Jessica. His eyes blazed like fiery brimstone. She could almost hear bugles sounding and the syncopated beat of a drum—Or was that her heart laboring under the stress of possibly losing another contract? She assured herself that its heavy thudding had nothing to do with the giant sitting across from her.

An unwelcome memory superimposed itself on the visual image of Grant McDougal. Her eyes narrowed in pain as Nicky's wiry frame, like an elongated shadow, came into focus. As a teen-ager she'd been an avid reader of Margaret Mitchell's *Gone with the Wind*. Nicky's physique and his southern-gentleman manners had matched those of Ashley Wilkes. Within moments of meeting him, she had developed a king-size crush, which made her easy pickings for the scoundrel. Nicky had played the role magnificently. And just as Scarlett had finally rejected Ashley, so had Jessica rejected Nicky. Unfortunately, Nicky had seen the handwriting on the wall and had made a few monetary plans of his own. But for Jessica, at twenty-five, there was no Rhett waiting in the wings—only debt, disheartenment, and disillusionment.

Jessica blinked her eyes rapidly to dispel the image.

"Batting your eyes in my direction won't work," Grant informed her.

"What?"

"I said—"

"The lemonade is here." Rose smiled at the sparks flying between her son and the attractive contractor. "Sweet and tart. That's the secret of the recipe. Satisfies all the taste buds and quenches the thirst."

Jessica studied the secret smile on the older woman's lips. She'd seen a similar smile on the faces of mothers as they gleefully presented their darling sons with a suitable woman.

19

Did Rose McDougal want a swimming pool or a daughter-in-law?

Evidently, Grant knew the answer, since he muttered a low warning: "Mother."

Rose shrugged innocently. "I guess you're unhappy with me."

"We've discussed this pool business on several occasions."

"I signed a contract."

"Lawyers can make mincemeat of contracts."

Grinning, Rose primly smoothed her skirt over her knees. "Your own lawyer drew up the contract."

"Kenneth knew about this?"

"Of course. We spent several hours discussing how he and his family enjoy their pool."

Jessica noticed the meaningful emphasis on the word *family*.

"Don't confuse the issue. I don't care if this yard is the only yard in Charleston without a pool. I don't want one installed here."

Jessica observed the exchange like a spectator at a Ping-Pong match. Grant was hard, tough, and commanding. His voice was deep and raspy, as if he'd been a heavy smoker at one time. The chiseled features of his face were too angular to be handsome. His tall and well-built physique caused Jessica to reconsider her first impression, that his muscles had been developed by lifting weights in the local gym. Much as she hated to admit it, he looked like a man who worked hard for his living.

"You have nothing to fear," Rose promised Grant, interrupting her thoughts. "The pool is shaped like a

V, with the deep part in the center. I'll be perfectly safe."

Jessica's mind raced ahead of the argument. Why did Grant consider a pool hazardous? Had there been a tragedy in his past related to water? Couldn't he swim? The thought of this strong, muscular specimen of manhood wildly flailing in water brought a smile to her lips. Maybe Grant McDougal wasn't as invincible as he appeared to be.

"That's what every victim of drowning thinks before they get into the water!"

Grant leaned forward, drew his thighs up next to the wicker chair, and placed his elbows on his knees. An unruly lock of golden red hair fell forward. Jessica noticed the sprinkling of freckles across the back of his hand as he impatiently pushed his hair back into place. How dare those strands of hair become disarrayed without his permission! Jessica mused, the corners of her mouth raising into a broad smile.

Noting the cocky grin on Jessica's face, Grant said, "You also know what I think about swimming pool contractors. They're the renegades of the building industry."

Her jaw dropped as Jessica's mouth opened to defend her trade. Rose turned toward Jessica to explain, but Grant's hand sliced through the air, silencing his mother.

"No pool!" The final edict came with a sharp slap to his knee.

"Now, Grant, stop worrying. My goodness, you're treating me like a child! I know my capabilities and the restrictions that age has imposed on me. You're a sweetheart to be concerned"—the charming pitch of her voice didn't change one iota as she staunchly restated her intention—"but I'm going to have a pool built."

"Not while you're living alone."

Rose beamed a proud smile from her son's face to Jessica. "Grant lives on Kiawah Island. He has a lovely home near the beach. Actually, it's on Surfsong Drive." Shivering delicately, Rose added, "It backs up to a lagoon filled with hungry alligators. We had a slight disagreement. I insisted on living in the historical district of Charleston rather than in a posh swamp."

"You don't have any business living by yourself." The reminder of his previous lost battle strengthened Grant's determination to break the contract with Plantation Pools. There were a multitude of pools on the island—perhaps his mother would reconsider moving in with him.

Jessica sensed that Grant resented her presence during their disagreement. Playing the role of mediator, she directed his attention back to the pool issue. "There are several safety features designed especially for your mother."

"Not interested," Grant declined.

She'd tried to be fair, tried to be reasonable, tried to help the enemy, and he'd rejected her kindness with curt, negative response. Silently, she shot daggers at Grant. Aloud, she sweetly continued listing the safety features. "In addition there are absolute restrictions banning four-legged prehistoric reptiles from the vicinity of the pool."

"The signs on Kiawah forbid teasing the alligators. That warning includes the two-legged variety, too,"

Grant snapped. "As for your architectural drawings, burn them. Mother isn't going to have a pool. If she wants to swim, I'll make other arrangements." Grant laced his fingers together and squeezed tightly as if the gesture would reinforce his determination.

Drawing the potshots back to her direction, Rose said, "I've given Jessica a check for the down payment."

"Let her cash it and watch it bounce from here to high heaven." Grant smiled grimly.

"Bad checks are illegal. You wouldn't want your mother to go to jail, would you?" Rose smiled benignly at Jessica, completely unruffled. "Do you happen to know if the penitentiary has a pool for the inmates?"

Rising to his feet, Grant flexed his arm, making all ten knuckles pop rudely. "I'll cover the check, but—"

Jessica reached forward and spontaneously hugged Rose. "In that case, we'll proceed as scheduled. I'll be here first thing in the morning with the backhoe."

"Over my dead body," Grant decreed.

Smiling her most charming smile, Jessica replied, "I'll look forward to seeing you."

She politely thanked Rose for the lemonade and got to her feet. Casting her a conspiratorial wink, Jessica pursed her lips. Remembering that ladies don't whistle, she clamped them shut and hummed the beginning notes of "Dixie."

CHAPTER TWO

When Jessica heard Grant bid his mother good-bye, her humming died as if she'd eaten a box of salty crackers. During the exchange of verbal ammunition, Jessica had remained relatively quiet, letting mother and son barrage each other. Evidently, Grant considered her to be the weak point in his mother's position and now planned to outflank his mother's defenses.

Picking up the unused stakes lying on the ground, Jessica waved one of the red flags in his direction. She wasn't going to surrender this contract. She needed it.

"Why don't we discuss our mutual problem over dinner?" Grant suggested.

His hasty invitation surprised him as much as it did Jessica. He'd felt the tug of physical attraction between himself and a woman on other occasions and had ignored it. For years, business commitments had required his undivided attention. But there was something about this pint-size package of dynamite that made him want to light her fuse and enjoy the fireworks. Without questioning the whys and wherefores, he let his instinct for spotting something special dictate his actions.

"No, thank you." He wasn't going to disarm her with good food and a bottle of wine.

Grant shoved his hands into his pants pockets. "No excuse? A belle usually makes some sort of polite excuse when refusing a gentleman, doesn't she?"

"My dance program is filled," Jessica quipped, dangling her wrist as if a formal dance card hung from it.

"I specialize in intermissions" came Grant's smooth retort. "Perhaps a cooling cup of planter's punch?"

His dark blue eyes flowed over her, but Jessica saw a dangerous glint sparking from the dark centers. Dangerous enemy, she thought, wondering if she could convert him to her way of thinking.

"You aren't married, are you?" Grant inquired, taking advantage of her momentary indecisiveness.

"Divorced."

His head nodded as if he'd gained an insight. "Plantation Pools was part of the final decree."

Jessica thrust her chin forward. "Plantation Pools belonged to the Hayes family long before—"

"I didn't mean to pry," Grant disclaimed when he saw twin flags of anger spreading across her high cheekbones. Realizing that he wanted to know more about this feminine enigma, he added in all honesty, "Well, maybe I should admit to being curious about you. Building swimming pools isn't exactly the occupation a Yankee associates with southern belles."

"Relegating southern women into stereotyped roles would be a tactical error. We're as liberated as our northern counterparts."

"Why construction work?"

"I'm certain *you* expect women to pound typewriters instead of stakes. Sorry I don't fit the mold, Mr. McDougal. I'm certain you'll understand my declining your invitation." She glanced down at her be-

25

smirched jumpsuit. "Let's just say I'm not properly attired for dinner."

"No problem," Grant said, ignoring her jibes at his male chauvinism about how a woman should earn a living. "I'll follow you home and wait while you shower."

"Give up, Mr. McDougal. I'm not going to dinner with you, and I'm not going to renege on building your mother's pool." Jessica spun away from him.

"Running away?" Grant inquired, chuckling lightly.

"Retreating to regroup my forces for a major skirmish at dawn," Jessica quipped. She disliked the way his rough voice stroked down her back, causing goosebumps on her forearms.

"I'll be here," Grant promised with ominous pleasure.

She checked him a quick salute as she climbed into the cab of her truck and met the challenge. "So will I, Yank. So will I."

She started the truck and carefully backed out of the abandoned driveway that ran parallel to the length of the McDougal yard. "I'm not afraid of him," she muttered, swiping icy fingers across her arm.

After turning the truck toward the highway, she silently repeated her statement. She'd learned to avoid cowardly behavior by expecting the worst possible outcome. What could Grant McDougal do to her?

She had a valid contract. His mother's check had already been deposited into her account. The earthmoving equipment would arrive as scheduled. There wasn't anything he could do to stop her.

"I've spiked his cannons," she said aloud, liking the

image. But saying it and knowing it to be the truth were two different matters.

Grant McDougal wasn't the type to ride off into the sunset with his six-shooter empty. He'd be back.

Her slim fingers clenched the steering wheel as she wondered what new tactic he'd try. Mentally she ticked off those he'd used: belligerence, anger, reasoning. And one last one—charm—made her momentarily breathless.

She wanted to deny that he had an effect on her, but she couldn't. "So?" she muttered. "He's attractive—so what? You've been around attractive men before without melting into a puddle at their feet."

He's different, her mind silently replied.

"Different? He's like nine-tenths of the men in the world. He thinks women belong in the kitchen or the bedroom."

Now you're getting closer to the truth.

Jennifer shook her head to dispel the thought of Grant McDougal in a bedroom. The image held.

"Hormones!" she explained. "I'm a normal, healthy, red-blooded woman!"

Without a man.

"Who needs a man? I've had a man." She corrected herself. "I've been *had* by a man. That's the legal limit for me!" she forcefully blurted.

She flicked on the radio and turned it to her favorite low-country radio station to drown out her thoughts.

Concentrating on the road and the music, strumming her fingers on the wheel, she passed the city limits sign posted on the Ashley River Road. Live oak trees draped with wispy Spanish moss and interspersed with pines and palmettos made a living can-

27

opy. She'd traveled down this road thousands of times, but for her, a feeling of days long gone always changed the blacktop highway into a sandy road used by horses and buggies.

Turning into the oak-lined drive leading to her home, she leaned forward, anticipating the welcome sight. Small dwellings built of century-old handmade bricks lined the road outside the main gate. Jessica reached up to the truck's sun visor and pressed the button on the control box that opened the wrought iron gate. She slowed the truck.

By modern standards, the house was small. It wasn't a huge mansion with Doric columns like those popular in films about the South, but it boasted wrap-around porches, which made it distinctive. Floor-to-ceiling windows allowed the sultry, fragrant breezes that blew in off the marshland to cool the house. And a red tin roof was a stamp of Carolina uniqueness. She loved the house and the ten acres surrounding it. That was all of her inheritance that the Hayes family had managed to keep.

Jessica parked the truck in back of the house. Plantation Pools had made it possible to make the costly repairs that were necessary during her father's lifetime, but during the past eight years since his death, since Nicky's frivolous expenditures, the house had suffered.

Jessica climbed from the truck, glancing at a shutter in need of repair. *Genteel poverty,* she thought, giving a southern name to the plague that had blighted her family tree. In a most unladylike manner she silently cursed her present financial status. She would need both the McDougal contract and a commercial pool contract to net enough money to tend to her home.

Her thoughts slipped back to the man who obstructed her. Grant McDougal wasn't the only man who scorned her occupation. Her father had abhorred her interest in construction and had completely dismissed her mechanical aptitude. He'd sent her to a fancy women's college to prepare her for a teaching career. Well, Dad, Jessica mused, a teacher's salary wouldn't even begin to maintain this piece of southern history. Much as she loved her father, he had been fallible. He'd given his blessing to her marriage to Nicky, thinking Nicky could run the pool business better than she. Although she missed her father dreadfully, she was glad that he wasn't around to see the mess she'd made of her life.

For a moment her shoulders slumped under the weight of her responsibilities. Maybe, like Rose McDougal, she was residing in the wrong place. There were plenty of newcomers in the Charleston area who would pay a pretty penny for the house and the small amount of acreage surrounding it. Maybe she should sell and move to a new house that wouldn't require much upkeep. Maybe . . .

Refusing to let herself slip into self-pity, Jennifer's spine stiffened with resolution. This wasn't the first time a Hayes had faced financial hardship. She wouldn't give up. Whatever it took to support herself and her home, she'd do it.

With that thought firmly implanted in her mind, she entered the front door and crossed to the kitchen. She'd eat, get a good night's sleep, and be ready at the crack of dawn to fight Grant McDougal.

* * *

Bright and early the next morning, Jessica headed back toward Charleston. She'd phoned the backhoe operator and the dump truck driver to make certain nothing would go amiss. Grant McDougal was going to witness the smooth operation of an experienced contractor, she promised herself with tight-lipped determination.

She arrived at Rose's house at seven o'clock, on schedule. Jessica coiled her long blond hair, caught it in a rubber band at the crown of her head, and settled a pale gray hard hat squarely on top.

"Hi, Harold," she greeted the operator. "Ready to dig?"

The short, stubby operator grinned as he rubbed the stubble of whiskers on his chin. "Yes, ma'am. I figure one day ought to do it, since none of the big trees have to be removed."

"Be careful. We want to disturb the present landscaping as little as possible." Glancing toward the abandoned driveway, she saw a dump truck lumbering over the ruts. "Good. Here comes Bubba. I'm going to stick around for a while to get you all started, then I'm meeting the plasterer over at the Herman house."

As the two men discussed the best way to position the backhoe and the dump truck, Jessica kept an eagle eye on the veranda.

Where was he?

She would have bet a bowlful of grits that Grant McDougal would be here pestering them with a million questions. Hopefully the drawbridge that connected Kiawah to Charleston had gotten stuck again and he'd been stranded! If only it would stick permanently, then he'd never arrive! She grinned to herself at the thought.

She decided that she'd better warn Rose about the upcoming commotion in the backyard and crossed the lawn to the door. She rapped on the screen.

"Mrs. McDougal? Rose? We're here."

"Come on in," a low, smoky voice invited.

There was no mistaking who had issued the invitation. Jessica could feel the hairs at her nape curling toward the husky sound.

"I expected you to be outside, drilling us with a multitude of questions about digging the pool," Jessica said as she stepped from the glaring sunlight into the screened veranda. She choked back a gasp as her eyes adjusted to the change of light.

Dressed in silk pajama bottoms, Grant stood peering through the screen. Slowly, as if he greeted her every morning in this state of deshabille, he said, "Help yourself to coffee." He motioned toward a silver pot nestled on a warmer.

"Uh, perhaps I'd better get back to the job," Jessica replied, unable to stop the blush that was creeping up her jawline.

"Mother insisted I serve you coffee in reparation for my harsh words yesterday."

Wanting to accept the coffee, she was acutely aware of the rust-colored hair that spread over his broad chest to the drawstring at his waist. Jessica shifted from one foot to the other.

Grant held his china cup and saucer toward her. "I'll have a warm-up."

The smile that broadened on his face told her that he was fully aware of his effect on her. His request that she wait on him diminished any gloating on her part. She bit her tongue to keep from telling him to get his own coffee and what to do with it. A splash across his chest would warm him up!

"Does my lack of circumspect clothing bother the modern-day southern belle?" Grant teased.

"I've been married, remember?"

"You're used to living with a man who sleeps in the nude." Grant shrugged without moving the level of the cup extended toward her. "Mother's sense of propriety demands that I wear something."

Unable to look him in the eye, Jessica focused her attention on the least-threatening object in front of her: the cup and saucer. "Cream? Sugar?" she graciously asked.

"Black. This coffee is a bit weak for my taste, but it'll have to do."

Jessica eyed the thick brew in the bottom of his cup and knew why he had so much hair on his chest. Stronger coffee would have had to be stirred with a concrete mixer. She filled his cup and one for herself, careful to dilute hers with several dollops of thick cream.

It pushed her powers of concentration to the limit to hand him his cup and saucer without a telltale rattle. "The excavation should be finished by this afternoon," she stated, diverting their conversation toward a relatively safe topic.

"Two, maybe three days, if you're lucky."

"Mr. McDougal—"

"Grant."

"I prefer to be on a last-name basis with my clients."

"You call my mother Rose."

"She's a woman!"

Grant pulled a chair from the table overlooking the backyard. "You call female clients by their first names and male clients by their last names. Interesting," he commented.

She settled into the proffered chair. "Customary business practice." She sipped her coffee, scorching her tongue.

"Another southern anachronism?"

"If you like," she conceded.

"That's interesting. I've been doing business with southerners for a decade and haven't experienced such formality."

"Okay, McDougal," she snapped in an imitation of his northern twang. "Satisfied?"

"Removing your hard hat would be a step toward satisfying me," Grant mockingly suggested as he lifted it from her head.

Her silky blond hair uncoiled and spilled over her shoulders. She felt his fingertips touch the confining rubber band as if he were considering further satisfaction.

"Don't."

"One step at a time," he muttered under his breath, a wistful expression on his face. Grant eased himself into the chair beside her.

"What makes you think it'll take two or three days?" she demanded, adroitly switching the conversation back to business.

He was mesmerized by the weak rays of sunlight that came in through the screen with just enough light to make her near-white strands shine. His fingers itched to remove the rubber band. "Less than a minute."

"McDougal, the best backhoe operator in Charleston can't dig a pool in a minute."

Grant cleared his throat. "Your backhoe will start digging in less than a minute is what I meant. Why don't you stop him?"

"Stop him? Are you crazy? I have every intention of completing this contract."

"That's a switch. I made a few phone calls after you left. Plantation Pools is great at digging holes, but they never complete a project within thirty days."

Her cup clattered against the saucer. "Some pools take longer than expected," she responded evasively.

Grant laughed at her understatement and blew on his coffee. "One pool took nine months to complete."

"We had unforeseen problems."

"Why don't you tell me about them?" Grant encouraged, leaning toward her.

Her blue eyes sliced through him. "I've provided you with one laugh for the day. Isn't that enough?"

"I wasn't laughing at you. The understatement you made is a classic in the construction business."

"What do you know about the construction business? The last thing you built was probably a sand castle at the beach."

"I know enough to see that your truck driver is going to hit the side of the garage unless—"

The sound of metal raking against wood jarred Jessica to her feet. Within seconds she was outside, waving her arms and shouting at Bubba, "Stop, dammit!"

The operator cupped his hand around his ear to hear over the sound of the diesel engine. "What?"

34

Jessica made a slicing motion across her throat to signal Bubba to cut the engine.

"What's wrong?"

"You're going to knock the garage down if you hit it any harder!"

Bubba glanced over his shoulder. "I thought it was the limb of that oak tree raking against the bed of the truck." A curt expletive and a quick apology burst from his mouth as he rounded the side of the truck.

"My exact sentiments," Jessica muttered. "Get in and cut your wheels sharply to the left. Ease away from the garage."

"You'd be better off if you'd—" Grant said, as he came up snapping a pair of pants into place.

"With all due respect, McDougal, I'm running this job. Cut 'em to the left, Bubba."

The dump truck edged forward. The bed was less than an inch away when Jessica heard a cracking noise overhead. "Stop!"

The crook of a major tree limb was pressing against the inner edge of the truck bed. Bubba opened the cab door and stepped out onto the running board. "I'll have to back up."

"Lift the bed, then pull forward," Grant curtly instructed in an authoritative tone that brooked no argument.

Seeing the wisdom of his strategy, neither Bubba nor Jessica refuted his suggestion. Raising the bed of the truck was such a simple solution. Why hadn't she thought of it? Shaken by the minor accident, she had overreacted. Embarrassed that Grant, a know-nothing pencil pusher, had saved the tree and the garage from further damage, she took several steps backward and lashed out, "Any further damage is your responsibility."

"You're welcome," Grant clipped when the truck inched forward.

Darn it, she silently blasted. "I would have—"

"Demolished the garage and done major damage to a two-hundred-year-old oak," Grant predicted with quiet accuracy. "Want to tear up the contract now or continue with this farce?"

"Farce! I built twenty pools without incident until you came on the scene. You're making me nervous!"

Grant simply smiled at her confession.

Never had Jessica wanted more to indulge in that century-old custom of southern ladies—to soundly slap the arrogant face of a man who was infuriating her. Stomping her feet and screaming seemed like a good idea, too. But she masked these urges with a strained smile that she hoped was a reasonable facsimile of being charming.

"I'll have the garage repaired, but the limb has to be removed."

"The contract stipulates that removal of any trees, shrubs, and bushes must have the owner's approval."

"I'll talk to Rose."

"You'll talk to me. I'm the owner."

"But—but—"

"You're backfiring," Grant teased.

"I'll wheelbarrow the dirt myself if necessary rather than ask for your approval on *any*thing."

"You were right earlier. It isn't going to take two or three days to excavate this pool. If you haul the dirt from the yard by hand, it'll take three or four weeks." Her flushed face entranced him. But he was unable to gallantly allow her to hack down the tree. He asked, "Is stubbornness a trait of southern womanhood?"

She heard him whistle "Yankee Doodle Dandy" as he pivoted and strode jauntily toward the house.

"Oh, no you don't," she gritted, hot on his footsteps. "I don't remember any paragraph in the contract with that stipulation. That's unreasonable. I'd have to have permission for every blade of grass that I removed."

Grant kept walking.

"You can't hold me to that section of the contract," she blustered, and grabbed his arm as he reached for the screen door handle. Grant shook her hand away as if she were a bothersome pest.

"Care to negotiate?" he offered, holding the door open for her to precede him into the house.

"You aren't interested in negotiating. From the beginning you've been against your mother having a pool. Deny it, you—"

"Yankee?" Grant lightly patted her bottom. "Why do southerners constantly forget who won the war? Are you still saving your Confederate money in case the South rises again?"

"I sold mine to a northern speculator!"

At her unexpected response, Grant tossed his head back and hooted with laughter. "You're priceless."

Jessica pursed her lips to keep them from joining him in his unrestrained laughter. Even as a child, she'd never been able to watch someone laugh without echoing their peals with her own.

"Come on, laugh. How about a smile? You have to admit my attorney is pretty slick."

"This isn't funny. Completing this pool on schedule is important to Plantation Pools."

"One smile from you might convince me to tell you how to get the dump truck into the backyard," he bargained, continuing to smile.

"If you know a way to do it, what makes you think I don't?"

"Because I have secret information unavailable to certain luscious southern belles."

"If you were a gentleman, you'd reveal your secrets without bargaining for smiles," she retorted, straining to keep her lips straight.

"I haven't claimed to be a gentleman. I'm a tough, insensitive Yankee, remember?"

"Your description, not mine."

"I'm also a mind reader."

"Hmph!"

"You wanted to slap my face and stomp and scream less than five minutes ago. Right?"

Jessica couldn't stop her lips from quirking upward on one side.

"Close?" He stepped forward and lifted her chin. "Your smiles are dangerous, little belle. They make me want to see if they taste as good as they look."

Her blue eyes rounded as his head tilted and slowly descended. His hand curved and cupped her chin, touching the sensitive skin on her throat, making her pulse pound erratically, making denial impossible. She wanted his kiss.

In the second before his lips gently settled over hers, she questioned her sanity. Why was she allowing this? Grant McDougal was the direct opposite of the Ashley-type men who normally attracted her. McDougal could almost pass for a redheaded Rhett Butler. At all costs she should be avoiding this kiss.

Her lips parted beneath his.

A small, almost inaudible groan slipped from his mouth into hers as he claimed her sweet breath. His muscular arm wrapped around her waist and lifted her from her feet, silently imploring her to entwine her arms securely around his neck. For long timeless seconds, he kissed her almost-sealed lips. As he strung a moist line of nibbles across her jawline to the vulnerable flesh below her ear, he whispered, "The driveway will support the weight of a loaded dump truck."

Aware that her enemy had revealed a valuable secret, Jessica thanked him by drawing his lips back to her own. Was she being a traitor to her own cause? The thought vaguely crossed her mind, but the sweet tenderness of his lips extinguished it.

CHAPTER THREE

Grant slowly lowered Jennifer to her feet. Shaken by her response and by the way his blood seemed to thicken and grow heavy as it pulsed through to each nerve ending, he searched her eyes for an explanation.

He scrutinized her lovely face. Bewilderment and confusion were erased as she tilted her stubborn chin, but the hurt lurking in the depths of her eyes made his heart wrench. Instinct told him that she'd been hurt by another man—badly.

"Make that two laughs that I've provided you with this morning," she said stiffly, turning her face away from his close perusal. "Don't bother sticking around for the third laugh; you'll be late for work."

"Jessica, I'm not laughing. You aren't either. I saw pain in your eyes. Who caused it?" Grant whispered. His large hand moved to frame her face.

Her eyelids lowered as she tried to hide her vulnerability. Grant bent, tenderly feathering his lips against the shadow her lowered lashes made on her cheeks.

"That story would really make your sides ache with laughter."

"I doubt it."

Gentle sincerity linked with the gentle strokes of his fingers breached the wall of silence she'd maintained about her ex-husband. Her lips parted, but bitter words clogged her throat.

Grant sensed her reticence. "Have you told anyone about him?"

With a mirthless chuckle, she answered, "No need to. Everyone knew what was going on long before I did. Haven't you heard the old saying about the wife being the last to know?"

She backed out of his arms. Her heart slammed against her ribs like a jackhammer breaking concrete. Taking a deep breath, she forced her curled fingers to relax. Until Grant McDougal barged into her life, she had blocked Nicky from her mind, not giving him a second thought. Was it her unrequited love for Nicky that was now making her heart feel as if someone were drilling through it? Reflexively, she shook her head. Nicky wasn't the cause of this sensation. Grant was. Oh no, she silently groaned, don't let me fall for him!

"How long have you been divorced?"

"Three years, thank God. If he'd hung around much longer, I'd be totally bankrupt." She leveled her eyes on Grant. "Remember the report about Plantation Pools digging holes that never held anything more than rainwater?"

Grant nodded.

"It should be updated. Those pools weren't completed in thirty days, but I did complete them." Pride in her accomplishment made her shoulders straighten. "Those and eighteen other pools. I turned Nicky's failure into my success."

His eyes held hers, then skated down her petiteness. "How could a little thing like you take on a man's job?"

41

"Nitroglycerine comes in small packages," Jessica replied, feeling as if she'd explode from the heat lasering from his eyes. He was going to devastate her senses completely if she didn't move away from him. She willed herself to step backward, but the lazy circles his thumbs drew on her upper arms kept her feet rooted to the spot.

His grip tightened on her momentarily. "You're still in love with him," Grant stated rather than asked.

Her lids shot open. She stepped backward. "No! Nicky destroyed any illusions I had about love. I'm my own person."

"No room for another person?"

"No," she whispered, responding to what her head, rather than her heart, advised her to say. She'd learned her love lesson well. Women who followed the dictates of their hearts were extremely foolish. Either foolish or immature, Jessica added. Heartache either kills or strengthens. In her case, she'd grown stronger and wise beyond her years.

"Not even on a less permanent basis? Say a weekend?"

A harsh sound parted her lips. "Comfort the divorcee? Is that what you're proposing?"

"You have to admit, there is a certain chemistry between us."

"Remind me to throw some sand on myself when I go outside to smother the fire."

"The fire burning inside me isn't going to be extinguished with a handful of sand."

Jessica picked her hard hat up from the table. "Stand under the dump truck when it unloads. Two tons ought to do the trick. I have enough problems."

"Your being dumped from this job is at the top of the list."

"Such finesse, McDougal!" she retorted with sarcasm. Steadfast in her resolution to avoid men—Grant McDougal in particular—she flipped her hair to the crown of her head and rammed her hat on.

"Did *he?*"

"Dump me? Like a ton of sand." Hands on her hips, she glared at him. "Is your morbid curiosity satisfied? Maybe you'd like to hear the gory details."

"No." The taut, angry angle of her chin showed the pain she'd bottled inside. Grant blocked her path to the screen door. "But I'm still not satisfied. I want you, Jessica Hayes. Not now. Not when you're looking for a whipping boy. But when you're ready."

The tight knot of anger she'd kept tightly coiled in her stomach unleashed itself at his blunt accusation. "Forget it. I'm not interested in whipping boys or overbearing men."

"You're interested," he confidently replied, capturing her wrist between his forefinger and thumb. "You're as interested as I am. The only difference is my honesty."

"Honesty?" Jessica scoffed. "I'm an expert on the subject. When my dear husband departed with another woman, I got a bellyful of honesty. I've had to work my tail off for three years to combat his *dis*honesty—professionally and otherwise."

"Sticks in your craw that he used you and damaged your business, doesn't it?" Grant baldly stated, knowing she needed to vent her spleen.

Discarding years of ladylike poise, Jessica snapped, "You're damned right." She jerked her arm away.

43

"Did you gain your vast wisdom through personal experience?"

"No. Building a business left little time for refined courtship."

"Then you'll understand my leaving this titillating conversation. I'm rebuilding, and that's tougher. Step aside, McDougal. I have a business to run."

"You're business is running," he said, twisting her words into the truth.

"My business is at a standstill until that dump truck is in your driveway, if that's what you mean. If you're insinuating that I'm running away from you, you're unbelievably egotistical."

"My ego is healthy. How about yours?"

"Just get the hell out of my way." Tears of frustration pooled in the corners of her eyes, making them a deep, unfathomable blue.

"Will an apology get me back in your good graces?" Grant asked quietly. "I owe you one for chipping away at that genteel facade you wear draped around you like a cloak."

"Just move! Your apologies are worse than your insults!" Unwilling to let him see the tears threatening to fall, she bodily pushed him aside and stormed through the door. "Bubba! Drive your truck around to the driveway! Mr. McDougal says it can take the weight."

"Okay, boss lady, but I've seen a lot of driveways crumble and owners sue contractors for replacement."

Jessica turned and caught a glimpse of a shadow moving from the veranda into the house. "Get moving. We have a pool to build."

Pushing thoughts of McDougal aside, she strode to the damaged garage to estimate the cost of repairing this morning's damage. It wasn't as extensive as she had originally thought. A bit of wood putty, a fresh coat of paint, and McDougal wouldn't have anything to complain about. She carefully loosened a painted splinter. Tucking it in the breast pocket of her jumpsuit, she decided to take it to the paint store to try to get a perfect match. Patching and painting one side of the garage would be less costly than painting the entire building.

As she watched the backhoe scoop a bucketful of sandy soil into the truck, Jessica momentarily wished that patching the hole in her life could be as simple. Kicking the soil with the toe of her boot, she grimaced. She didn't love Nicky. For months on end, between bouts of crying, she'd convinced herself that she hated him. But that was another example of her foolishness. She didn't love Nicky, but she didn't hate him either. *Indifference*—less volatile, less consuming, less draining—was the word she used to label her feelings.

Jessica removed a lace-edged handkerchief from her pocket. She wiped her brow and glanced at the sun peeking over the limbs of a huge oak tree.

"It's going to be a scorcher today," she mumbled to herself.

As she wiped her lip, she sighed. The heat from the August sun could never blister her skin with the devastating effect that one kiss from Grant had accomplished. Realizing that Nicky wasn't the cause of her reaction to Grant led her to draw a conclusion that she would have preferred to avoid.

McDougal's kisses disturbed her.

More than disturbed, she admitted, remembering

how his lips had expertly moved against hers. They aroused her to a fever pitch—a feat Nicky had never accomplished. Grant was as different from Nicky as day from night, so at least she couldn't fault herself for falling for the same bait twice.

She'd grown up with Nicky. Women had spoiled him rotten by catering to his every whim. Jessica hadn't been an exception to that rule. Not until she'd seen the traces of lipstick and smelled the cloying perfume did she open her eyes and take a hard look at her husband. Nicky was a selfish scoundrel. He had robbed her of her girlhood dreams and stolen from her company. Her only regret was that she hadn't saved her pride by kicking him out of her life before he ran away.

What was it McDougal had said about her? Something about the difference between the two of them being his honesty. She'd hidden the way that accusation had hit her like a doubled fist. There wasn't a dishonest bone in her body. In that respect, they were alike.

McDougal's honesty was threatening to strip away her shell of defense. He didn't mince words by disguising his intent with flowery compliments. He stated his objective, then with single-minded determination blasted through the barriers she put between them.

How do you fight a man who fights fair?

Unaccustomed to blunt honesty from men, she was drawn to the dazzling light of honor surrounding Grant. He clearly, succinctly expressed his beliefs— even if they were wrong, such as his assumption that she was still in love with Nicky.

His statement about her doing a man's job also offended her, but she knew exactly where Grant stood regarding women in the construction industry. Her knowledge of his attitude, combined with her building a pool for his mother, would have to be the emotional barrier protecting her vulnerability.

Grant McDougal was temporarily attracted to the velvet of the woman but not to the steel of the worker and the survivor. She was attracted to his honest strength but not his chauvinist attitudes.

Having restructured her defenses, Jessica circled the backhoe until she faced the driver. "I'm going to the other job. You can reach me there if you run into any problems."

The driver nodded, then waved.

Without realizing why, her eyes were drawn to the windows along the back of the house. One curtain was pulled aside.

"Let him watch," Jessica mumbled, briskly heading toward her truck.

Grant let the curtain fall back into place when he saw the Plantation Pools truck back down the driveway. Jessica would have blown a gasket if she'd known how close he'd come to stepping in and supervising the pool excavation. Granted, his expertise was more in high-rise buildings than in holes in the ground, but the same principles were involved.

He had spent his high school and college summers as a "gopher" in various trades. Now, armed with a civil engineering degree and the instincts of a gambler, he'd carved out a niche for himself in the building industry. For a second he wondered why Jessica thought he didn't know his butt from a hole in the ground about construction. Most builders knew his name and his reputation. The fact that she specialized in backyard pools rather than commercial pools was probably the reason. Actually, he'd read in the expression on her face that had slotted him as a high-rise executive. He'd been amused. She'd misjudged him.

Should he have set her straight about his line of work? Grant shrugged into his long-sleeved white shirt. When could he have told her? While they were screaming at each other last night? He would have sounded like he was beating his chest if he'd yelled, "Hey lady, I'm one of the biggest contractors in the Carolinas." He wasn't a man who tooted his own horn. Earlier, when he thought her men were going to change his garage into a carport, he'd been tempted to take matters into his own hands by offering to drive the dump truck. And yet he hadn't. Why?

"Because you had better things to do with your hands," he said aloud, glancing at his hands as he buttoned his cuffs. "Like touching Jessica."

The memory of the porcelain texture of her skin sent a tremor through his fingers. She'd felt good— softer than he'd expected. He could teach her a few things about efficiently consolidating her labor force, but there wasn't a thing she needed to learn about kissing.

He raised his starched collar and wrapped a conservative striped tie around his neck. As he dressed, he mentally took off Jessica's gray jumpsuit and imagined her in whispering silks, sleek satins, and luxurious inches of lace. A full-length mink . . .

His eyes blinked. For a man who'd prided himself on carefully converting pennies into big bucks for capital investment, his fantasy bordered on the ludicrous

—as ludicrous as the possibility of seeing Jessica Hayes in anything other than work clothes.

Her refusing him stung.

He knew he wasn't a Robert Redford lookalike, but dammit, women seldom refused him. Patting his flat stomach, he reassured himself that he was physically fit. What else could be wrong? he wondered.

They'd argued over building the pool, but he'd given in once he'd read the contract. But not too gracefully, he amended. Maybe that was it. She called herself a lady. Maybe he wasn't a gentleman enough for her. Maybe she was one of those Charleston snobs who only associated with other bluebloods. What did she want? A wimp?

Picking up his briefcase, he polished his initials, which were inconspicuously engraved on gold plate beneath the leather grip. Could it be that she objected to him because he reminded her of her first husband? God, he hoped that wasn't the reason. But from the things she'd said and hadn't said, that was a logical possibility.

"Nicky," he spat. "What kind of man gets past third grade answering to 'Nicky'?"

Grant preferred to think of Nicky as a juvenile wimp rather than as a mature man. Not because he was afraid of hand-to-hand combat but because he didn't want Jessica's interest in him to be based on old memories. When he made love to her, he didn't want her thinking about another man.

The smile widened. Hell, here he was worried about what she'd be thinking about in bed, and he couldn't even get her to go out with him.

"Grant, you're going to be late," his mother called from downstairs.

"Coming."

He glanced at the mirror on the back of the door for a quick final inspection, then left the room with a purposeful stride. He neatly stored his thoughts of Jessica Hayes into the back of his mind and went briskly through the door and down the steps.

"Time for a quick cup of coffee?"

Grant kissed his mother's cheek. "I'm late."

"I thought you'd want to supervise the work in the backyard."

His mother's disappointment couldn't be dismissed. She seldom made demands on his time. "I've seen all I need to see for today."

"Did I hear voices coming from the veranda?"

"Jessica was here, but she's gone."

"Oh, I'd hoped to have a nice chat with her."

Glancing at his watch, Grant said, "I imagine she's at the paint store by now."

"My, she is fast. Are they ready to paint the walls of the pool already?"

Grant chuckled. "Pools are plastered, not painted," he corrected.

"Then why is she buying paint?"

"To repair the damage she did to the garage."

"Oh, dear. An accident on the first day. How disheartening for her. I do hope you consoled her."

"I offered what help I could."

Rose grinned, her eyes twinkling. "I knew you'd come around to my having a pool and lend a helping hand. Jessica's such a spunky little thing, isn't she?"

"A real spitfire," Grant agreed. "Do us both a favor and get that matchmaking look out of your eyes."

"Grant, you're thirty-two. It's time you found yourself a nice woman and settled down."

"You bulldozed me into letting a pool be installed. Don't you think that's enough for today?"

She wiped her hands on her frilly apron and looped her arm through the crook of his elbow. Then she nodded.

"I haven't changed my opinion about pool builders in general," he said. "The past reputation of Plantation Pools is a good example of why homeowners should be wary. Every hole dug and uncompleted is a pockmark on the entire building industry."

"But—"

Grant stopped his mother from defending Jessica with a wave of his hand. "Off the record, I'm glad you chose Jessica's company." He winked as he grinned down at the petite woman he dearly loved. "By the way, I met this retired—"

"Now who's playing matchmaker? You've already paraded half a dozen Civil War relics through my parlor."

"I don't want you to be bored." He kissed her as he left the house.

Rose smiled secretly. "Oh, I won't be, dear."

She watched Grant wave through the window of his Porsche as he backed out of the garage. "I plan to provide us all with a great deal of excitement!" she said aloud to herself. Yes, indeed! She'd passively watched Grant bury himself in his work to build his financial empire, and now the time had come for her to stick a hornet's nest under his foundation!

51

* * *

Jessica pushed the button on the beeper hooked on her belt. She asked the paint salesman if she could use his phone.

She dialed her business number and waited impatiently for the ring.

"What's the problem, Louise?"

"Mrs. McDougal has called several times. You'd better get over there with smelling salts."

"What happened?"

"The backhoe operator is hacking down an oak tree."

"What?"

"I couldn't believe my ears, either."

"I'll take care of it. I'll check back later."

Jessica slammed the phone back into place and rushed through the door. First the garage, now the tree. She silently groaned. Darn it, those men are experienced!

In record-breaking time Jessica was back at the McDougal house. She expected to see huge branches being hauled to the abandoned driveway for the trash men. She climbed from her truck and entered the yard. The backhoe operator smiled and waved. Jessica motioned to him to shut off the engine.

"What's going on around here? I just got a call from Louise saying you're butchering tree limbs."

"A twig or two." The burly man gestured toward a low branch. "It kept sticking me in the neck, so I broke it off and threw it over there."

The twig lying beside the mound of dirt was no more than four inches long. Baffled, Jessica picked it up and signaled for the operator to continue digging. She dashed down the walk that led to the veranda.

"Mrs. McDougal!"

Rose stepped to the screen door and opened it. "I'm glad you're here. I just talked to Grant. He said for you to stop your crew until he gets here. I fixed chicken salad for lunch. Won't you join me?"

Tossing the twig aside before she entered, Jessica dug her fingers into her scalp. Now she was certain she'd stepped down the rabbit hole and was talking to the Queen of Hearts. "Did you call the office with a complaint?"

"Do you like your chicken salad stuffed in a home-grown tomato or on freshly baked bread?"

"Tomato." She followed Rose into the kitchen and raised her hands palm upward, beseeching a straight answer to her question.

"Yes, dear, I did phone your office once or twice."

"Louise said—"

"Such a nice phone voice Louise has. Mayonnaise?"

"Where are the limbs?"

"Limbs? Oh! I must have exaggerated a mite. Sometimes I do that when I'm trying to reach important people."

Jessica collapsed into a kitchen chair. "I envisioned the trunk of the tree hacked to pieces."

"You should have heard the high-pitched squeals of that snippy little woman Grant has for a secretary. She assumed you'd cut down every tree in historic Charleston." Rose covered her mouth to stifle a girlish giggle. "She said—"

"You called Grant with the same complaint?"

"Of course. My dear, he does own this property."

"And he's on his way over here to throttle the person responsible?" Reflexively, her hands moved to protect her throat. She audibly groaned and added, "I hope Grant looks before he leaps or, in this case, strangles."

"You aren't afraid of him, are you?"

"Nobody with an ounce of sense would want to meet him on a battlefield. My great-granddaddy backed the South when the odds were against him. He lost. I hope I'm not fighting a losing battle, too."

Rose wrapped her frail arm around Jessica's shoulders and gave her a quick hug of reassurance. "You may lose a few minor skirmishes, dear, but I'm certain Grant will ultimately wave the white flag of surrender."

"You want me to win?" Jessica asked doubtfully.

"Of course. I really do want a pool."

"Then why did you complain to Grant?"

Rubbing her hands together, Rose crossed to the kitchen sink. "I'll start the toast for Grant's sandwich. He hates tomatoes."

"Rose!"

"Shall we eat on the veranda or here in the kitchen?"

"Rose!" Jessica repeated.

"I think the veranda. That way you can supervise your crew." Rose brushed her hand across her forehead. "I do believe I'm getting a headache. Would you mind fixing the sandwich? I think I'll go to my room and rest."

"Oh, no you're not. You called Grant. You're going to be the one who explains about the tree."

"But dear, you wouldn't let Grant scream and yell

54

at a poor defenseless old woman with a headache, would you?"

"Something tells me Grant has never raised his voice in your presence," Jessica replied when she spied a smug smile on Rose's face.

"No, but there have been times when I thought he'd burst a blood vessel." Holding her temples, Rose moved to the kitchen door. "Trust me, Jessica. I know what I'm doing. I believe those are the same words you used before I agreed to build the pool, aren't they?"

Jessica nodded, then shook her head. "You've forgotten one detail. You signed a contract with me because you wanted a pool. I didn't sign a contract for matchmaking services, because I don't want a man. Arranged marriages went out of style along with the horse and buggy."

"Isn't it a shame?" Rose concluded as she stepped from the kitchen into the hallway. She paused and tossed over her shoulder, "A nice moonlit ride around the Battery would be nice. Perhaps . . ." Her voice trailed off as she turned the corner.

Her forehead propped in her hand, Jessica muttered, "She's nuttier than a southern pecan pie! Worse! She's a romantic nut!"

Jessica jumped to her feet. She wasn't about to let Rose manipulate her into her son's arms. She'd build the pool, and she wouldn't be bamboozled into anything not specified in the contract.

She strode quickly from the kitchen and hightailed it out of the house. She made a mad dash for the driveway where she'd parked her truck. Heaving a sigh of relief, she hastily started the engine, goosed the gas pedal, and put the truck into reverse. She glanced in her rearview mirror a second too late. Her foot hopped from the accelerator to the brake.

Metal struck metal.

There wasn't a doubt in her mind as to who owned the shiny black Porsche she'd just creamed.

CHAPTER FOUR

Jessica tempered her impulse to get out of her truck and abjectly apologize to Grant by remembering her father's sage advice about a car accident she'd had when she was sixteen. Back then, she'd admitted the accident was her fault. "Always figure a way to make it the other driver's fault no matter what," her daddy told her. "If at all possible, have the other driver arrested."

Good advice, but hard to follow, she thought as she glanced in the rearview mirror. McDougal sat in his car, glaring through the windshield. His mouth moved, but she couldn't make out what he was saying. That's probably for the best, she concluded, biting her lip.

She dismounted from the cab. Slowly, she walked to the rear of her truck and inspected the steel bumper that had smashed the Porsche's headlights, grill, fenders, and hood. Other than a dark smear of black paint, her truck wasn't even scratched. She glanced surreptitiously at McDougal as he opened his door.

"Eight . . . nine . . ." he growled ominously.

"Ten," she chimed, thrusting her chin forward aggressively. "You ought to have better control of your vehicle."

With one foot on the ground, he stopped. "Eleven . . . twelve . . ." Counting to ten hadn't been enough for him to gain control of his temper. The audacity of the woman! She backs into his car and coolly blames him! "Thirteen."

"Speeding up the driveway, weren't you?" she challenged.

Grant exploded from the car. "You little hellcat!"

"Don't call me any pet names," Jessica calmly derided, shoving her trembling hands into her pockets so McDougal couldn't see how he intimidated her. His blue eyes blasted her like a Gunite nozzle. A hundred pounds of pressure per square inch threatened to drive her to her knees. She met his glare. Her chin threatened to wobble. Stiffening her upper lip, she tilted it higher.

His hands clenched and unclenched as Grant ground his teeth on the number fourteen. Didn't she even know that her stubborn chin raised at that angle was an open invitation? If she were a man, he knew exactly what he'd have done to lower it.

"I hate to do this, but I think we'd better call the police." For protection, as she noted the way his chest heaved as he gulped drafts of air into his lungs, she tacked on, "I don't want to press charges—"

"Press charges!" Grant thundered, pushed beyond control. It snapped. He grabbed her shoulders and shook her. "Press charges? Lady, you're a menace! My car was *parked!* You blithely plowed into it!"

Through the haze of red clouding his judgment, he saw her wince. He released her, spun on his heel, flexed his hands, then he rammed them into his pants pocket. Until now, he'd never touched a woman vio-

58

lently. As angry with himself as he was with her, his throat worked up and down in an attempt to calm his fury.

Jessica was unbalanced by being shaken like a rag doll, then deposited on her feet. She clung to the high fender of her truck. Whatever smattering of guilt she felt about hitting his car had evaporated. How dare he manhandle her! One swift kick at the back of his knees would bring him down a notch or two. As if he'd heard her thought, Grant glanced over his shoulder, daring her to do her worst.

She watched his broad shoulders shudder. He impaled her with his icy blue eyes as he slowly walked to his car. Without a word, he got in, started the engine, and cautiously backed down the driveway. Only his hands, knuckles white as they gripped the steering wheel, indicated the thin thread of control he maintained.

Jessica threw caution to the winds when she saw him departing. "Leaving the scene of an accident is a felony. Don't expect my insurance to pay for the repairs."

For half a second, the powerful Porsche hesitated. Then gravel spat from beneath his rear wheels. Still in reverse, Grant careened the sports car backward.

Jessica stood her ground until he disappeared. Although his silent withdrawal indicated a victory for her, she felt like a sniper in a tree. "A snake in the grass," she muttered—her actions had been so low.

"What's going on?" Bubba asked from the other side of the wooden fence. "You okay, boss?"

"Yeah," she answered from between tight lips.

Bubba hoisted himself up until he could peer over the fence. "Did I hear something hit your truck?"

"A minor fender-bender," Jessica answered, minimizing the damage when she saw concern on the operator's face. "Nobody's hurt."

"You're white as a ghost. You sure you're okay?"

"A bit shaken up." She grimaced, remembering the force of McDougal's hands on her arms. Casting Bubba a weak smile, she strode the length of the truck.

The fault was squarely on her shoulders. She'd hit McDougal's car. She'd goaded him with her defensive ploy. And she knew she'd been wrong. Her keen sense of fairness demanded she do everything in her power to correct that situation. Not even Bubba's backhoe could dig a hole deep enough to bury her feelings of guilt. "I'll be over at the insurance office. Call Louise if you run into any more problems."

An hour later, Jessica wondered how much her insurance rates would be raised by her admitting to being the cause of the accident. Her major problem, money, raised its ugly head. She'd have to devote all her energies to completing the McDougal pool and work on the bid for the commercial pool that was sitting on the drafting table at the shop.

But her immediate problem—to pacify Grant McDougal—had top priority. She wouldn't let her insurance agent contact him. And easing her conscience by paying for the damages wasn't enough. She owed him an apology.

By now, she reasoned, he'd have had time to cool off. She glanced at her watch as she climbed into her truck. She was tempted to procrastinate, but she started the engine and headed back to Rose's house.

His mother would have his business telephone number. Her lips twitched into a wry smile. Rose undoubtedly had it memorized, from the number of times she'd dialed it today.

Jessica dreaded the questions Rose would ask. Would the old-fashioned matchmaker tease Jennifer for calling the man, or would she dial the number herself?

In order to avoid returning to the scene of the accident, Jessica parked the truck on the street. Mentally she rehearsed what she'd say to McDougal as she climbed the front steps and rang the doorbell.

She'd be crisp, businesslike. A simple apology would suffice. After all, he had shaken her until her teeth rattled. No groveling was necessary.

The door swung open. Her blue eyes rounded. She expected to see Rose's smiling face but was momentarily stunned by the sight of copper-colored chest hair —peeking through a half-buttoned shirt—at the height where snowy white head hair should have been. Summoning up her last few ounces of courage, she raised her face and smiled.

"McDougal. I'm glad you're here. I dropped by to get your phone number from your mother."

"Excitement has taken its toll. Mother's upstairs resting."

"Since you're here, I won't have to bother her." Jessica shifted from foot to foot. Through the screen door she couldn't read his eyes. Was he still angry enough to throttle her? He hadn't welcomed her warmly, but then, she could hardly expect an open-arms reception.

Grant pushed the screen outward. "Won't you come in?" he said with polite formality.

"That won't be necessary," she replied, hesitant to enter the house with Rose asleep upstairs. Self-preservation, an instinct that couldn't be ignored, warned her to tread carefully—backward. "I'm sorry I hit your Porsche. My insurance will cover the damage," she babbled, edging toward the steps. "I've got to"— her tongue flicked over her lower lip and captured the too-revealing word *Run!* before she pronounced it— "get going."

"Come on in, Jessica. Your business is here, in my backyard, remember?"

She gestured in the direction of the driveway, which led to the backyard. "I'll go around—"

His hand circled her wrist and pulled her forward. "I have a few things I want to say to you."

"I apologized!"

"But I didn't accept your apology, did I?"

Jessica dug her heels into the throw rug covering the polished heart-of-pine floor. He released her wrist so suddenly, the rug almost slid from under her feet. She recovered her balance, and his large hands took hold of her upper arms.

"I'm not a pepper shaker. Don't shake me again," she gritted between thinned lips.

She clamped her fingers onto his biceps as if her strength matched his. The hard muscles bunched, then relaxed, as his hands fell to his side. His raised hand directed her toward the formal parlor. As her eyes followed his palm, she felt his other hand nudge her in the small of the back.

"That's what I wanted to discuss with you."

"Pepper shakers?" she asked, scolding herself for not keeping her eyes on both his hands. She quickened her pace to alleviate the tingle running up her spine.

"Apologies."

She glanced over her shoulder in time to see his blue eyes twinkle. That generated another charge of electricity. He placed his hand on the curve of her waist.

"Um-hm," McDougal hummed. He gestured for her to sit down on the sofa, but she remained standing. "I'm certain you expect one."

Expect one? An apology was the last thing Jessica expected. A slow torturous death was the first. And somewhere in there was another tongue-lashing.

His fingers grazed below her ribs. She raked her tongue over the roof of her mouth to distract herself from his enticement. Dry. Cottony. Her wavering look moved from his seductive eyes to his slightly parted lips.

"Redheads are known for their tempers." One hand raked through his thick hair as if to remind her of the color. "Ever since I was a kid, when I was taunted by little blond girls calling me carrot-top, I've prided myself on keeping my cool."

"Sparks fly every time we see each other," Jessica said in a husky voice that she barely recognized as her own.

"I wonder why?" Grant murmured, taking her shoulders in his hands—the same shoulders he'd shaken earlier.

"I provoke you?" she whispered.

"You are provocative," he agreed, altering her meaning.

Her ears buzzed with the tension between them. "I'm building a pool you don't want?"

"I want the builder, not the pool," he corrected. His head slanted, slowly lowering.

"I smashed your car?" Her head tilted as her voice lilted upward.

"And my equilibrium."

"You should hate me."

"I should hate what you're doing to me."

His lips curved over hers before she could ask why they didn't hate one another. They should. They had every reason to. Jessica closed her eyes. The sweet, coaxing tip of his tongue traced the bow of her lower lip, leaving no room for reason. He teased her mouth with butterfly strokes.

Jessica looped her hands behind his neck. She wanted his kiss—a *real* kiss. A sigh escaped from between her lips as her breasts flattened against the wall of his chest. It threatened to ignite the spark of passion that Grant held in check. He drew the sweet fleshy bow of her lip between his, gently suckling.

"What am I doing to you?" Jessica mouthed against his lips in a breathy whisper. His lips dropped to the sensitive curve of her neck. Her knees threatened to buckle as the tip of his tongue made forays around the shell of her ear. She knew she should have been asking herself, What is he doing to me? Her head tilted to give him easy access as she ignored her silent query.

"This," he replied, pulling her even closer. "Pushing me to the brink of my self-control."

Jessica swallowed. He'd answered her question. "Then we'd better stop," she weakly suggested, turn-

64

ing her lips to the base of his neck, peppering it with tiny kisses.

"Ummmm."

"Was that a yes or a no?" Her fingers spread over his collarbone. Of their own accord, they strayed to the sharp point of his starched collar, then to the knot of his tie. It bobbed as his long fingers spanned her hips and drew her to him.

"No. Open your lips. Let me inside you."

She hesitated, jarred by his frankness. He rocked her hips against him. A melting sensation that she'd long forgotten made her lips part in a small gasp. He parted them further as his tongue boldly took her mouth. She'd wanted his kiss, a real kiss, but his masterful strokes caused shafts of unwanted desire to course through her. The velvet rasp of just his tongue against hers was more erotic than lovemaking with Nicky.

The surfacing of that subconscious thought made her heart turn over. Reflexively, she pushed against McDougal's muscular shoulders to free herself.

"Stop. Now. No more," she pleaded between sharp pants. Her fingers fluttered helplessly over her reddened lips.

"Dammit, Jessica." His hands moved to frame her face to keep her from turning away. "You let him get between us, didn't you?"

"No," she denied, too quickly.

Her eyelids tightly squeezing shut told Grant that she'd lied to protect herself. "Don't lie to me. Were you wishing it was your ex-husband kissing you? Wanting you?"

"No!" She felt his hands weaving through her hair

to her scalp, demanding that she open her eyes so he could see the truth. She complied. "Your kiss scared me."

"Why?"

Jessica's flushed cheeks grew pinker. "Because . . ." She couldn't tell him that his kisses by themselves inflamed her senses more than making love with Nicky had.

"Don't give me a lame excuse. I want the reason, Jessica. The truth about why you panicked."

"Let go of me," she stalled. "I can't think when you're breathing down my neck."

"Lady, I don't want to give you any room to wiggle out of the truth. You're going to give me an honest answer." Beneath his palms he felt her jaw muscles go taut. She was girding her defenses. "Please?"

She could fight aggressiveness defiantly, but the change in the tone of his voice when he spoke the last word shattered her defenses. "I liked kissing you too much."

Her confession wrung McDougal's heart. He brought her face to his chest. "Oh, Jessica. What am I going to do with you?"

"We'd both be better off if we left each other alone" came her muffled reply.

"I don't think that's possible. Do you?"

She shook her head. "Darn it, McDougal. I'm building a pool you don't want. My employees tried to demolish your garage. I wrecked your car. Why me?"

"I have to admit it, my life hasn't been boring since you pounded those flags into the backyard."

"Now who's being evasive?" The luxury of being

wrapped in the warmth of his embrace gave her the security she needed to match his boldness.

"I'm not certain you're ready for square shooting."

Jessica knew she was playing with dynamite, but his kiss had already lit the fuse inside her. "Why me?"

"I want you, and I think you want me every bit as badly. Am I right?"

Inwardly, she squirmed against his forthrightness. She'd been brought up to skirt around the issue of desire. But somehow, cushioned against McDougal's chest, with her nose inhaling his masculine fragrance, the forbidden topic intrigued her. "That depends on what you mean."

"Specifically?"

She nodded, wondering if he'd become as tongue-tied as she would be if asked the same question.

"I want to kiss you at my leisure. Long, slow, drug-ging kisses that would have made your feminine ances-tors swoon. Right now, I can feel the tips of your breasts through my shirt. I want to see them, caress them, taste them." McDougal heard her take a quick breath. "I want you to explore me while I'm exploring you."

"That's enough. I get the picture."

"Oh, no, my little prude. You asked me what I wanted." He eased her onto the sofa. "I won't let you go running out the back door."

"You're scaring me again." Jessica felt her back touch the overstuffed arm of the sofa.

"My kiss scared you because you liked it too much. Are you liking what I'm saying too much?" He shifted her into one arm. His free hand moved to cup her breast. His thumb raked over her hardened nipple. "Does this scare you? Or do you like it?"

"Please, McDougal."

"I *am* pleasing McDougal. This is what I want, remember?"

"That's not what I meant."

His thumb agilely flicked open the button of her jumpsuit. His fingers moved inside her lacy bra. "Scared?"

"No," she answered truthfully. "I want—" She couldn't make her mouth form the words. She unbuttoned two more buttons, then unfastened the front clip. The slow massaging pressure of his hand never stopped.

"You want my mouth kissing your breasts. Say it."

"Kiss me," she compromised. She shrugged her shoulders free of clothing. "Here."

McDougal lowered his arm to her waist, arching her until his lips flared around her nipple. His lips, tongue, and teeth gorged themselves on her sweetness. "You taste like wild honey," he said, moving to the other puckered tip.

Jessica pulled his head tighter to her breast. As he teased and tasted, she felt shock wave after shock wave of longing ricochet from her sensitized breasts to an aching place deep inside. As if McDougal felt it too, his hand followed a descending path until it rested on the source of her longing.

She lost all sense of time and place. Caught in passion and desire, she reacted instinctively. Her hips arched, her lips parted when he claimed them. Their tongues mated again and again. She heard small kittenish sounds, but she didn't realize they came from the back of her own throat.

Grant echoed her moans. Touching her was like holding a blue flame. The taste of her seared itself on his mind. Want built into need. He desperately needed her. He'd had enough experience to know that he was dangerously close to making love with her on his grandmother's brocade sofa and that he didn't give a damn about the consequences. The only thing that held him back was knowing Jessica would never forgive him if someone walked in.

He warred within himself. Each kiss was more frenzied. He hadn't touched her yet—not the way he wanted to touch her. He needed to bury himself inside her, feel her legs lock around his waist, hear her sweet cries of ecstasy as she reached the pinnacle of their lovemaking.

Sounds from overhead—the box springs squeaking, bare feet moving to the chair—ended his internal battle. In too few precious minutes he knew he'd hear footsteps on the staircase. He couldn't do what they both wanted and needed. He had to end this delicious torment one way or another.

His hands shook as he began to rebutton her jumpsuit. "Jessica, come with me."

"Yes," she whispered from her spiraling passion. "I want you. Please."

"Sweetheart, I can't." Frustration put a sharp edge on his tone.

"What?" Her hands covered the backs of his. It was then that her senses cleared enough to realize there was fabric between her breasts and his hand. "What's wrong?"

"Everything." He looked up at the ceiling. "Wrong time. Wrong place."

"Wrong woman?" she asked, adding to his list of wrongs. She straightened, removing his hands. The magical spell he'd spun around her shattered.

"No! Nothing on this earth could have stopped me if we'd been at my place." He moved onto the sofa beside her and extended his hands, palms upward. "I'm shaking all the way to the soles of my feet."

Jessica heard a door upstairs opening, followed by noises on the steps. "Nap time is over."

"She'll be down here any moment. Drive me to my place."

"Rose just saved us from getting carried away." A wry smile curved her lips. Her legs were shaky, but she stood up from the sofa.

"Fine. Carry me out to my place, and we can get carried away there."

Rose stepped into the parlor. Her eyes twinkled with mirth. "Did I hear you asking Jessica to carry you?" She winked at Jessica and confided, "Grant didn't start walking until he was two years old because he preferred being carried around."

"Mother!" Grant groaned, rising to his feet.

Rose sighed dramatically. "Some things never change. Why would you want Jessica to drive all the way out to Kiawah when you have a perfectly good car of your own?"

"I gave his car a little alteration with my rear bumper," Jessica said, minimizing the damage.

"Two accidents in one day? Oh, my dear, you weren't hurt, were you? You look a bit feverish."

Almost three accidents, Jessica corrected silently.

And the last one would have been the most damaging. Rose's waking up at an opportune moment had saved her from the most disastrous of the three—her son.

"I'm fine. I dropped by this afternoon to tell Grant that the insurance would take care of everything and to check on the excavation in the backyard. I was just leaving."

"Don't rush off. Grant, did you offer Jessica any refreshments?"

Grant opened his mouth to answer, but Jessica took Rose by the crook of her arm and answered dryly, "He certainly did. Why don't you come with me and see how your pool is coming along?"

"Grant?" Rose looked over her shoulder. "You're the expert. Aren't you coming?"

For a split second, Grant didn't know whether he was coming or going. And as a man who prided himself on following the straight path to success, that bothered him. He heard Jessica ask, "Expert at what?" and waited for his mother's answer to fall like a hatchet on his neck.

"Building things," Rose said, watching Jessica's head swivel ninety degrees to take another look at Grant. "Grant is president of the Northern Contractors of America. Son, didn't you tell Jessica who you are?"

"I didn't have a chance." From the way Jessica narrowed her eyes, he knew he wasn't likely to ever get another unless he did some quick thinking. As much as he wanted to continue what they'd started in the living room, the withering look on her face signaled that she wouldn't even consider being alone with him again unless it was for business. He hated to dangle his business connections like a carrot in front of a stubborn mule, but Jessica's tight-lipped expression gave him little choice. "Tonight I'd planned to talk to her about doing the pool at the new hotel complex being built near the airport."

Rose patted Jessica's hand. "Oh, my dear, that would be a plum of a job."

A plum? Or a carrot being dangled, Jessica wondered, kicking herself for not having recognized Grant's name or noticing his familiarity with building contracts and dump trucks. She'd assumed he was a know-nothing pencil pusher even when everything pointed in the other direction. He hadn't concealed the truth. She'd simply been obtuse—her fault, not his.

"We could discuss the project during the drive to Kiawah."

"Don't let him ramrod you into something you don't want to do," Rose advised. Her eyes glistened with glee as she threw down the gauntlet between her son and Jessica. "He's a wily Yankee, and you're a—"

"Renegade," Jessica blurted, quoting McDougal's description of pool builders.

"—genteel southerner," Rose said, generalizing their differences to challenge both of them.

Jessica graciously acknowledged Rose's compliment with a smile. Rose could afford to be mistaken. Jessica couldn't allow herself such a luxury. Subcontracting for Northern Contractors of America could put Plantation Pools permanently in the black. First and last, she had to be a businesswoman.

"I'll take you," Jessica said.

Grant heard the underlying steel in her offer. She'd

do the taking, not the giving. He grinned as he silently altered her intent. They'd both be taking, both be giving. Otherwise, whether making love together or doing business together, they'd both fail.

CHAPTER FIVE

"You could have told me you're a contractor," Jessica said after they'd inspected the pool site and were getting into her truck.

"And here I thought you resented my telling you anything," McDougal said, a hint of amusement in his voice. "Your *taking* my advice isn't likely, is it?"

She started the engine. With utmost care she backed down the driveway. "You're about to give some. Advice, that is. Aren't you?"

"I'm tempted, but I'm battling the temptation."

"Is this personal advice or professional?" She turned the truck and headed toward the Maybank Highway.

"Professional."

Jessica worried the inside of her cheek. "Does it have anything to do with building your mother's pool?"

"Partially." Grant twisted on the bench seat in an effort to get comfortable. The seat was the right height for Jessica to reach the gas pedal, but Grant's knees jarred against the dashboard with each dip in the road.

Jessica was silently debating whether to give Grant the satisfaction of listening to him, but she saw his predicament, too. By the time they reached Kiawah his spine would resemble a pretzel. Southern hospitality included seeing to the comfort of her guest. She pulled over to the side of the road and stopped. "You'll be more comfortable if you drive."

Surprised, Grant asked, "You don't object to me being in the driver's seat?"

"Just keep your eyes on the road and your hands on the wheel," she stipulated, "and your advice to yourself."

After they'd switched places, Grant said quietly, "You've overlooked something regarding mother's pool. Jessica, let me help you."

"Plantation Pools doesn't need your help building backyard pools, thank you very kindly. Commercial pools are another matter. What do you think my chances are of getting the bid on the hotel pool?"

"Experienced out-of-town builders make the competition tough. They have streamlined operations."

"I do, too." She watched his eyebrow fly upward in skepticism. "The garage and your car will be fixed! Those were minor accidents that won't affect the completion of the pool."

"Minor but costly. A series of small accidents can break a company."

"I can do the job," she huffed, contrary to the evidence he'd witnessed, contrary to the past reputation of Plantation Pools. She leaned against the door, crossed her legs, and folded her arms over her chest. "We did get the pool dug today. We are on schedule."

"Not for long," Grant muttered to himself, glancing at the clouds forming over the branches of the trees. Reading her withdrawn body language, he asked, "The subject of pool-building is closed?"

Behind her tight lips Jessica ground her back molars. She nodded curtly.

Her eagerness when she talked about her work made Grant acutely aware of how much he wanted her. He wanted to see that same look on her face for him as a man, not as a general contractor. He wanted the same sense of anticipation that lit her face, that drove her to take risks, for himself.

After a few minutes of silence, Grant turned on the radio. Music to soothe the savage beast, he mused, as her eyes tried to bore holes in his tough hide. Less than an hour ago, before his mother's untimely interruption, Jessica's eyes had shimmered with passion. He had to remember that to keep the chains on his temper.

He hadn't meant to touch her, but he had barely been able to stop once he had. She'd never know how much effort it took now to keep both hands on the steering wheel.

Jessica watched the play of light and shadow from the oaks lining Bohicket Road on McDougal's profile. Light accentuated the hollows under his cheekbones and highlighted the gold strands in his hair. Darkness softened the determined thrust of his chin and the aloof tilt of his head.

Raw power, she thought. She had little difficulty imagining him on a multimillion-dollar job site. Bubba had snapped to attention when McDougal had given him an order. Men could smell power. Women were fascinated by it.

She blinked, unwilling to admit being fascinated. Aggravated? Yes! Infuriated? Definitely! Fascinated? No, no, no, she told herself.

Liar!

"Are you in a hurry to get back to Charleston?" he broke into her thoughts.

"I'll drop you off, then head toward home."

"Care to join me for dinner?"

"Thanks, but . . ." She gestured toward her uniform.

"No problem. I'll call and have the restaurant pack a basket." He looked overhead. A gully-washing rain would wreak havoc on the freshly dug hole in his mother's backyard. Dammit, he wanted to tell Jessica to have her men shore up the sides or cover it with plastic, but she'd bluntly told him to mind his own business. "Are you certain you have nothing more you need to do on mother's pool today?"

"Positive. Tomorrow the reinforcement rods will be laid. The next day the plumber will install the pipe. Everything has been carefully scheduled."

"Sometimes accidents aren't always caused by employees," he hinted. Mother Nature had a way of destroying construction schedules, too. "We'll have to picnic at the house. It looks as if it's going to rain."

Jessica smiled. McDougal seemed to be fighting their mutual attraction as much as she was. He'd invited her to dinner, then given her an excuse to refuse. She wasn't going to be accused of running again. She'd show him she wasn't a coward.

"Do you usually invite someone to dinner and then tell them they have work they should be doing?"

"Usually it's the other way around. I refuse dinner invitations because of my work load."

"Is that why your mother plays matchmaker?"

Grant nodded. "Arranged marriages have romantic

77

appeal for my mother. Her great-grandmother was a mail-order bride. I'm surprised she hasn't placed an ad in the paper—'Single male, 32, businessman, looking for southern belle.' "

"Somehow that doesn't sound as romantic as being a mail-order groom, but I guess the principle is the same. A person looking for a mate advertises for what they want. Maybe that's more sensible than falling in love."

He turned left on the road to Kiawah. Gray clouds, heavy with moisture, rolled in off the Atlantic. As they crossed the wooden bridge over Kiawah River, he noticed the tide was high.

"Are you serious?"

"Louise, the woman who works in my office, regularly runs an advertisement in the local paper," she said. "She says she's tired of singles' bars and waiting for Mr. Right to magically appear on her doorstep. By sifting through the responses to her ad, she feels as if she has control of her life, instead of letting herself be swayed by romantic notions or physical appeal."

"Sounds like she's encouraged you to do the same."

"She has."

"You haven't." Grant based his conclusion on Jessica's attitude toward men. From what she'd said, Jessica wasn't interested in men, period. "Do me a favor. Don't let Louise talk to Rose. I don't want her writing any ads for me."

Jessica grinned. "Who do you think Rose talked to when she called my office to report the limbs being shorn from your oak trees?"

"First thing tomorrow, I'm going to stop delivery of the paper to her house."

78

"Why? As creative as your mother is, I'm certain she could write a very appealing ad." She chuckled as she considered suggesting the idea to Rose. Keeping Grant busy answering ads could be preferable to having him supervise building the pool.

"Jessica," Grant said, smiling, "don't. Mother has enough zany ideas without your helping her."

The guard at the entrance to Kiawah motioned for them to stop. Grant gave him the information necessary for a temporary visitor's pass.

"Think the guard will be able to keep the hoards of women at bay when your ad appears?" Jessica mischievously teased.

"If I start getting mysterious calls, Ms. Hayes, I'll run an ad for you, and then you'll need that guard's brother to keep the men away from your house." The amusement in his eyes ruled out any force from the threat. "On second thought, I'd have to find another method of retaliation. If your front door is guarded I won't be able to come courting."

Jessica turned her face toward the side window. His blunt statement of his intentions sent tiny fingers of pleasure up her spine. He'd lured her into driving him home by showing a willingness to discuss the bids on the commercial pool. This hardly fit her image of old-fashioned courting, but perhaps it was a modern-day twist. Mail-order brides were out of fashion, now replaced by females advertising. Perhaps instead of roses and candy, he'd give her the pool contract?

She matched his directness by saying, "McDougal, I'm interested in building pools, not meaningful relationships."

"Keep saying that, honey. A big lie has to be repeated to make it believable."

Jessica caught his glance and held it. "Why don't you offer me the contract and see what happens?"

"At this stage, offering you the contract wouldn't prove anything. Ladies don't play bedroom games to get contracts. By the same token, ladies don't show gratitude by—"

"I get the point," she interrupted Grant, and her ears turned beet red.

"Ladies have a code of honor. Honest businessmen have a similar code. Don't confuse the boardroom and the bedroom."

"I may not be as scrupulous as you think I am."

Grant grinned. He was tempted to reach over and pat her knee. "Successful businessmen take risks based on instincts. After Nicky ran off, you could have bankrupted Plantation Pools and not worried about finishing his contracts. The local people wouldn't have held it against you. But you didn't. At great cost, you protected your reputation."

"Family pride was at stake. My dad built the reputation of Plantation Pools," Jessica explained.

"That's one of the reasons."

"That *is* the reason," she argued.

"Initially, family pride motivated you to complete those contracts. Strong people hate failure. By changing your ex-husband's business failure into a success, you got rid of the guilt you had about failing in marriage. Right?"

"I wouldn't admit that to my best friend," she answered. His astuteness amazed her. He'd put his finger right on the heart of the driving force behind her work. By proving to herself that she could right the wrongs Nicky had done, she had proven her own self-worth.

"I'm certain you wouldn't. You're probably wondering how I figured it out, aren't you?"

"Yes."

"Placed in a similar situation, you did what I would have done. We may hail from opposite sides of the Mason-Dixon Line, but we still fight fair." He lifted her hand to his lips. "There's one difference in where you are now and where I'd be."

Her fingers curled around his palm. "What?"

"After I proved to myself that I was strong—wounded but not crippled—I'd be ready to try again. You're still running scared."

She lightly squeezed his fingers. "I'm here with you."

"False bravado. I scare you to death because you know I'm not faint of heart. I want you, Jessica Hayes, without the gray ghosts from the past."

They slowed down at the guard gate for the private section of Vanderhorst Plantation. A huge raindrop splashed on the windshield. Then Grant gunned the gas pedal. Jessica's past experience had left her hurt from her ex-husband's unfairness. Tonight Grant planned to show her that she could trust him. She'd refused his help, but she was going to get it anyway.

Jessica barely heard the thunder booming overhead —the pounding of her heart was louder. Grant had made his intentions clear. He wanted her. His silence challenged her to think about the ghost from her past and decide what she wanted.

Could she put her failures behind her and say the

old ghosts were dead and buried? Did she want to nurse her past grievances and forsake the brightness that the future could hold? It would have been easier for her if he had made empty promises about the contract instead of being so honest and straightforward about his intentions.

"We'd better make a run for it," Grant said. He parked the truck as close to the front steps as possible. Grabbing her hand, he pulled her across the seat as he opened his door. "This isn't going to be a summer shower."

Hand in hand, they made a dash for the steps.

Once inside, Grant ushered her toward the living room. "Go on in and make yourself comfortable. I have a quick phone call to make."

As he hurried off, she walked into a diamond-shaped living room with two walls of glass overlooking a large lagoon. The walls were separated by a magnificent fireplace made of white coral. Large ceramic pots held tropical plants. Her hand slid across the nubby cream-colored fabric covering the twin sofas. Casual throw pillows lined the back. She glanced over her shoulder. Large original pastels in shades of pale blue and green harmonized the view and the interior of the room.

She moved around the sofa, across the palest of green carpets, over to the floor-to-ceiling window. Rain peppered the lagoon. On the opposite bank, she could just make out the shape of an alligator slithering into the water. She shivered. An alligator in the backyard wasn't her idea of a pet.

McDougal entered the living room carrying a towel

for her to dry off. "How far are you from the beach?" she asked.

"Very close. You can get there on the bike path on the other side of the house next door."

"I didn't notice a house when we pulled in the drive," she commented.

"That's the beauty of Kiawah. You have the advantages of being secluded without the disadvantages of being isolated." He crossed to the bar. "Care for a drink?"

"Sherry, please, if you have it."

He nodded, selecting from his stock of liquor. "I understand why my mother prefers to live on the Charleston peninsula. She says it's like living in a slice of history. The slow pace accommodates her age. I like the architecture of those grand old houses, but I find the closeness confining. Out here, during the off season, I can go to the beach and stretch my legs without seeing a soul."

Jessica joined him at the bar. "Your home is lovely."

He handed Jessica her sherry and teased, "Including my mother's pet peeve—the alligator out back?" He liked the way her eyes warmed when she laughed. "He's there to remind the owners that Kiawah isn't really paradise."

"Along with the snakes, the no-see-ums, and the mosquitoes?"

"And gorgeous women who would rival the beauty of Eve," Grant complimented, raising his glass to touch the rim of hers. He toasted, "To a beautiful lady."

"And to a silver-tongued gentleman," she returned.

His bright, intense eyes seemed to be searching for hidden answers to questions he hadn't asked. Uncertain, she lowered her lashes. "Did you order dinner?"

"No." His head tilted in the direction of the windows. "It's raining cats and dogs. I have steaks in the refrigerator."

The phone rang as Jessica glanced over her shoulder. Raining cats and dogs! But a heavy rain would erode the sides of the excavation! "Does it rain here before it hits town?"

McDougal nodded. Picking up the phone, he put a restraining hold on Jessica's arm. "McDougal residence."

Jessica frantically scanned the room for her truck keys. If she hurried, maybe she could get back to the pool site in time to shore up the sides.

"Yes, Mother."

"That's Rose? Let me talk to her."

He shook his head.

"McDougal, give me the phone. Tell her I'll be there just as fast as I can."

"They're my men." Grant watched Jessica's eyes round in surprise. "No, Mother. They aren't installing a vinyl liner. There's a storm headed your way. To keep the sides of the pool from caving in, I'm having Casey and his crew cover the hole."

Jessica jerked her wrist from his loose hold.

"Jessica knows." McDougal listened to his mother, but his eyes dared Jessica to move even one muscle. "No, I don't want any more accidents to happen, either. The walls caving in could cause days of delay. Yes, Mother. I'll tell her not to take chances by rushing out into the storm. I'll see you tomorrow. 'Bye."

"Is rain what I overlooked? It's what you tried to warn me about, isn't it?" Jessica asked, feeling damned foolish for having rejected his advice.

"I heard the weather forecast while you were showing mother the hole." He shrugged, excusing her lack of preparedness. "This time of year, who'd expect a rain squall? It's one of those unpredictable flukes of nature."

"That quick phone call you made when we first arrived was to one of your foremen, wasn't it?"

"Yes."

"You could have said something to me. It's my job. My deadline."

"My backyard," he smoothly injected.

"Don't you know how this makes me feel? Like a first-rate amateur! Darn it, I've heard about jinxed pools, where everything goes wrong regardless of how meticulous the builder is, but I can't believe I've got one! I hate having someone else doing my job for me!"

"Would you rather redig the pool than accept my help?"

"Of course not!"

"Then what's the problem?"

Jessica groaned, clamping a hand to her forehead. "I swear this pool is jinxed."

"Want to cancel the contract and refund the down payment?" he asked, giving her an alternative he knew she'd find more distasteful than accepting his help.

Her back stiffened. "Is that why you didn't tell me about the rain squall? You wanted me to back out of the contract?"

"I haven't changed how I feel about having a pool in mother's backyard." He circled the bar. Standing directly in front of her, he reasoned aloud, "Shouldn't you be graciously thanking me for coming to your aid?"

She took a step backward. "Thanks wouldn't be necessary if you'd told me about the weather forecast."

McDougal closed the gap. "Perhaps I didn't tell you because I remembered how graciously you accept help. The driveway and the dump truck," he reminded her.

"I didn't kiss you because you told me about the driveway."

McDougal asked, "Why did you kiss me?" and she realized she'd fallen into a hole she'd dug herself.

Her eyes lowered to his lips. The forthright question demanded an honest answer. "Because I wanted to kiss you."

"Do you want to kiss me now?"

"I don't know," Jessica said, confused by the way her body leaned toward him of its own volition. Ten seconds ago, she could have pounded him for making her feel unqualified to build a pool. But now, in less than a flash, his nearness had quelled that urge.

"How long do you think it will take before you know?" His fingertips trailed over the hair on her shoulder. He could be patient. He'd learned years ago that anything worth getting was worth waiting for. Things obtained too easily were of little value to him.

"When we kiss, I get confused," she admitted softly. "I keep thinking I should avoid you like a bag of dead Gunite."

McDougal cocked his head, silently asking for an explanation.

86

"When dead Gunite is used to shoot the inside of a pool, nobody can tell from the appearance how weak the walls are. But when the owner empties the pool to clean it, holes start popping out from behind the plaster. Dead Gunite is just about the worst thing that can happen to a swimming pool contractor."

"Are my kisses the worst thing that can happen to you?" His large hands framed her face. One thumb lazily touched her bottom lip.

"They're devastating. I lose track of who I am, where I am, and what's going on around me. I was still in shock this afternoon when I showed your mother the pool—otherwise I'd have noticed the change in temperature. I'd have known it was going to rain."

Grant smiled at her delightfully candid confession. "The feeling is mutual. I kissed you, and I forgot we were in my mother's living room and that she was in shouting distance."

"At least you recovered soon enough to button my clothes," she said with a wry smile. "I'd have been thoroughly embarrassed if you hadn't come to your senses."

"Jessica, when we stopped, remember I said it was the wrong time and the wrong place?"

She nodded.

"Here. Now. It's the right time, the right place. I pressured you into bringing me home. I won't force you to kiss me. But I want you to kiss me very, very badly."

"You aren't making this easy," she whispered, raising on tiptoe. "I'd rather you pulled me into your arms and kissed me, leaving me without a choice."

His hands dropped to his sides. He smiled at her, a somewhat wistful smile. She didn't know that her taking the initiative was of the utmost importance to him. But he couldn't give an inch.

"No, honey. This is one choice you're going to have to make. Go after what you want, knowing it's what I want, too."

Her arms were heavy as they looped around his shoulders. "You aren't helping at all," she said, whispering her complaint.

"You'll have to tell me what you want . . . the same way I've told you."

Grant sensed that her reticence had changed to eagerness. He savored the moment, longing to see her excitement for him kindle sparks in her eyes as bright as when she talked about contracts.

Jessica felt the warmth of his breath on her upturned face. Quiet. Steady. Like the man, she thought. Solid as a rock and as unyielding.

"Bend a little," she instructed, her lips several inches below his. "I can't reach you."

She was reaching him—more than any woman in his life had ever reached him. The thought made his stomach muscles tighten. Jessica Hayes could ask anything of him and he'd do it. He wondered if she realized the power she held over him. For a second, he wondered if she'd use it against him.

Her first husband had taken everything and given nothing. She realized that McDougal would give everything, but that in return he wanted all of her. He wasn't the kind of man who would settle for second best. He'd demand everything, and he'd give everything.

Jessica slanted her mouth under his. Her kiss symbolized more than the touching of two mouths. To her, she'd taken her first wobbling step toward seeking affection from a man. She'd made the choice.

Beneath her hands she felt his powerful shoulders, but it was McDougal's inner strength that drew her close. He was a man who would be there to back her up, who would demand as much of her as he demanded of himself.

She ended her kiss, breathless from the discoveries she'd made. As McDougal, solid as his name, as solid as the foundations he built to support high-rise buildings, as solid as his reputation, was a man a woman could trust.

Neither of them heard the roll of thunder or saw the sizzling cracks of lightning outside. Palmettos bent and oaks swayed. Tropical rain pounded heavily on the roof overhead. But inside, nature was on a different course. Jessica clung to Grant until he swept her into his arms, burying his face in the curve of her neck and shoulder.

CHAPTER SIX

Grant held Jessica, holding his breath. He waited for the words that would have him carrying her from the living room to the bedroom. He heard a branch split, fall, and skitter across the balcony. Overhead, the lights silently flickered. Grant expelled his long-held breath.

"The timing is still wrong, isn't it?" he asked, loosening his bear-hug grip around her slender waist. Every cell in his body screamed denial of what he was about to say. "We can wait."

"Why wait?" Jessica mouthed against his feverish skin.

He lowered her to her feet and steadied her with his hands on her forearms. Grant gave her a long, steady look. "Because I sense that you'd wake up in my arms wondering what you were doing in my bed."

Jessica started to shake her head, then she let her chin drop.

"Come on, honey." He wrapped his arm around her shoulders. "I'll fix you a steak. By the time we've eaten, the storm will have blown over."

His ability to know her reactions before she did mystified her. "How do you do it?"

"On the charcoal broiler," Grant replied, deliberately being obtuse.

"My face must be like a road map," she muttered aloud. "You can see exactly where we're going, while I have trouble locating where we are."

"A little salt, pepper, garlic powder. Four minutes on one side, then—"

She lightly elbowed him in the ribs. "Hush, McDougal. I'm trying to figure out what happened."

"Nothing happened that you have to worry about." He contained his smile, but his eyes lit up with amusement.

"Nothing? One minute I'm stuck to you like plaster on a Gunite wall, and the next minute you're reading my mind, telling me what I'll be thinking tomorrow morning. That's *nothing?*"

"How do you like your steak?"

"Raw," Jessica growled, disoriented by the quick turn of events.

Grant caught her chin in the fork of his thumb and forefinger. "Medium rare," he decreed as if he really were reading her mind.

"Are you trying to be funny?"

"Would you rather I laid down on the floor and kicked my heels against the carpet to relieve my frustration?" he asked, half in jest, half serious.

"Only if I'm allowed to take pictures," Jessica quipped, regaining her equilibrium and her sense of humor. "Give me one straight answer, will you?"

"That depends on the question." Grant opened the refrigerator and selected two steaks from the meat compartment.

"Don't be coy."

"Men aren't coy. Southern belles are, maybe. Men? Never." He couldn't resist ruffling her feathers, distracting her from her objective.

Jessica sighed in exasperation. "You're avoiding my question."

"Not really. You want to know how I knew you'd be unhappy about making the choice to share my bed."

"Now you're reading my mind with your back turned toward me." She watched his economical movements from the refrigerator to the spice rack that was built into the side of the butcher block. He methodically seasoned one side of the steaks and then the other. "I'm not certain I'd have made that choice. I was still at the kissing stage."

"Ummm. And we both know where that leads, don't we?" His bold question was accompanied by a piercing glance that demanded a truthful reply. "Hand me a plate, please."

"Directly to the bedroom." Without thinking, she opened the cupboard to the right of the sink and got a plate. "But to my recollection, my thoughts were on the here and now, not the future."

Grant grinned. "How did you know where I kept the plates?"

"Doesn't everybody keep them right above the dishwasher?" She lifted her shoulders as she handed him the plate.

"Most people keep the glasses to the right of the sink and the plates in the next cupboard over. I don't because I'm left handed. The glasses are over there. The same way you knew where the plates were kept, I knew how you'd feel later."

"Intuition?"

"I was just a step ahead. Call it second sight. Call it putting myself in your shoes and finding my toes being pinched." He grinned at the thought of putting his size twelves in her size five shoes. "Whatever. I knew how you'd feel."

"Too bad you weren't tuned in to my thoughts when I put the truck in reverse this morning. You'd have saved the Porsche from a smashed front end."

"True. But on the other hand, you wouldn't be here if I'd parked on the street, would you?"

The absurdity of his logic tickled Jessica. She laughed. "Does that mean my insurance doesn't have to pay for the damage?"

"Fix the salad. I'll think about it while I'm outside on the screened-in porch grilling the steaks." He slid back the door, casting her a sexy wink. "Can't have me doing more than my fair share of the work, can we?"

The door slid shut before Jessica could think of a smart retort. She pondered the meaning of second sight as she crossed to the refrigerator and opened it. Two unmarked white drawers were underneath the bottom shelf. Without pulling out either drawer, she closed her eyes and tried to visualize what was inside. Lettuce. Tomatoes. Celery. Cucumbers. Carrots. Onions. She shook her head. No, no onions. Her eyes opened slowly, and she pulled out the drawer on the left side.

"So much for second sight," she muttered. She shoved the drawer, filled with potatoes and onions, back into place. She opened the other one and grinned. "Right stuff, wrong drawer," she hooted.

She gathered the necessary items and placed them on the butcher block. As she prepared the vegetables, she found herself intrigued by the notion that Grant McDougal could divine her thoughts. When they'd first met, she hadn't fooled him for a moment with her whopper about the pyramid. Of course, that was easily explained now that she knew he was in the construction business himself. Little stakes with red flags were a common way to mark a future excavation.

But not all his guesses were accurate. When she'd told him that she was divorced, he'd guessed that Plantation Pools was part of the divorce agreement. He'd also thought she was still hankering after Nicky. Knowing he'd made a couple of mistakes eased her mind. She'd rather think of Grant as being sensitive than being a know-it-all.

Grant rapped on the door to get her attention. "Steak's about ready," he said.

She grinned and gave him the okay sign. He turned back to the grill.

Under other circumstances, he'd have used the indoor grill. But fixing the steaks outside gave him a chance to cool off and gave Jessica some breathing space. Grant hunkered down to check the flame. The wind whipped through the screens and threatened to extinguish the fire under the grill, but the flames burning inside Grant burned a fiery blue.

He'd done the right thing, but knowing that didn't dampen his desire. Oh yes, he admitted ruefully, he still wanted her, and it took an effort to keep from charging into the kitchen and claiming her.

"I fixed the salad and set the table," Jessica said as

she stepped from the kitchen to the porch. "How are the steaks?"

"Charred on the outside, bloody on the inside," Grant answered, mentally likening himself to the steaks. "Just a little longer."

"It's stopped raining, thank goodness. The wind should dry the water on the cover your men put over the pool. You saved me a couple of days on the production schedule. Thanks."

Grant tightened his grip on the tongs he used to turn the steaks. He watched the thick skein of silky blond hair, held by a thick rubber band at the crown of her head, sway across the middle of her back. His fingers itched to touch it.

"My pleasure," he responded, lost in his sensual thoughts.

"I'm glad you aren't the pencil-pushing executive I had you pegged for," she said, smiling. "Why'd you choose the construction business?"

Grant chuckled. "I guess I'm what they call in the trades a natural-born builder. As far back as I can remember, I've been building things. I built my first skyscraper when I was six—out of Leggos. At ten, my treehouse was the envy of every kid on the block. While the other teen-age guys were bagging groceries and filling gas tanks, I started a fix-it shop to earn spending money." He tested the center of the steaks with the edge of the tongs. "One thing led to another. By the time I'd graduated from college with an engineering degree, I'd done everything from plumbing to painting, foundations to roofs."

"Do you still work with tools?"

"I've been known to sneak out of the office to drive a few nails," he admitted.

"Better to drive nails than bite them," Jessica quipped, understanding the stress that came with his job.

Grant nodded, placing the steaks on the platter. Jessica opened the door for him.

"What do you do when you're uptight?" he asked once they were seated at the dinette table. "Swim?"

"I don't have a pool."

"A swimming pool contractor without a pool? That's like a builder living in a mobile home." He made a tsking noise. "Wait till Mother hears about this!"

"Plantation Pools also installs spas," Jessica countered. "I don't have a pool, but I have a wicked spa."

"Wicked?"

She ducked her head, sliced a piece of meat, and poked it into her mouth to avoid explaining her slip of the tongue. Through her fringe of eyelashes, she saw McDougal's fork stop midway between his plate and his mouth.

"The steak is great," she said after she'd swallowed. "How's your salad?"

"That blush of yours is sexy as hell," Grant said, refusing to let her off the hook. "My imagination is running wild."

"I didn't ask you why your treehouse was so popular," Jessica blurted, revealing more than she intended.

He couldn't resist teasing her. "Ah, you're comparing my treehouse to your spa?"

"I'd like some ice water. Can I get you some?" Jessica hopped to her feet. "I saw some milk in the refrigerator—which would you rather have?"

"A beer would be nice. About as refreshing as skinny-dipping in a spa, wouldn't you say?"

"I wouldn't know," she lied. She went into the kitchen and rummaged in the refrigerator until her face felt cooler.

When she returned, Grant matched her lie straight-faced. "I lost my virginity in the treehouse."

"At ten?" She was holding the beer can in a death grip to keep it from slipping from her hands. "Precious little devil, weren't you?"

Grant caught her wrist when she put his beer on the table. "I lied."

She could tell he expected a similar admission from her, but for her, skinny-dipping and virginity weren't suitable topics for dinner-table discussion. As if he'd read her mind, he eased his chair back from the table and pulled her onto his lap.

"Your hands are cold, but your face is as red as a firecracker. Put your arm around my neck and tell me about being wicked in the spa."

Her heart racing, Jessica said primly, "Ladies don't sit on gentlemen's laps without a newspaper between them."

Grant's throat worked, almost strangling to keep from openly laughing. "Keep squirming like that, and you'll find out why."

"You are the most outspoken man I've ever met," she admonished, aware of his tense, powerful thighs. His hand rested on her hip as if it belonged there.

He pulled her arm across his shoulders. "Is that a complaint or a compliment?" he asked.

"Both. I like your honesty, but"—she began to relax and he nuzzled the side of her neck—"I'm used to men who filter their thoughts before they reach their mouths."

"And women who are inhibited by an etiquette book full of don'ts?"

"Um-hmm," she purred.

"Forget about filters and rule books. Tell me about the spa. Maybe I'll have you install one here."

She leaned against his muscular chest. Her eyes drifted shut as she pictured what kind of spa he should have. "Yours should be king-size. Sleek black marble. With a heater and an aerator." She felt a slight tug, and her scalp tingled as Grant freed her hair. "There's nothing like being submerged in a hot spa on a cold, clear night with bubbles of steam the only thing between you and the stars."

He combed his long fingers through her hair, loving the sensuous way it clung to the callouses of his palm. It smelled of sunshine and wild flowers. Living silk. Softer than a cloud. He trapped a low groan of desire in his throat. His voice was husky when he said, "Dark, cold night. Hot, bubbling water. Haven't you forgotten something essential?"

"Wine," she added. "Crisp and fruity. Served in a long-stemmed, crystal goblet."

"You attend the first pool party. Do you christen spas?" He coiled a thick lock between his fingers, then rubbed it against the whisper of a shadow on his jaw.

"I haven't."

"Would you?"

"I'm not part of the deal," she said. She had a sinking sensation in the pit of her stomach at the thought of McDougal sharing the intimacy of the picture she'd described.

"I'm sold. How long do I have to wait for installation?"

"That depends."

"On what?"

"Other bids. Contracts. Schedules. I don't promise anything I can't deliver."

His heart skipped a beat. Was she angling for the hotel complex job? He glanced down at her face, looking for the eagerness he'd witnessed earlier. He saw only guileless repose, and he was thankful she'd never learned the art of disguise. She reminded him of a small cuddly kitten he'd had as a child.

"Work me in, would you?"

Jessica blinked, then shifted off his lap. "Are you serious? You want a spa?"

"With a sales pitch like that, I'm surprised there isn't a spa in every backyard in Charleston."

"Do you think I should change my businesslike spiel?" She backed up when she realized his head was practically nestled between her breasts.

"Do, and you'll be on my lap again—face down— with me applying your rule book to your backside." His devilish grin took the sting from his threat. "By the way, don't worry about a thirty-day clause on that contract. I like the idea of your spending a lot of time on this job site."

"Where do you want it?" Jessica forgot the rest of her dinner as she strode back into the living room. "You could extend the screened-in porch and put it there. That location would be terrific if you decided to have a spa party."

"In the wintertime, when the leaves are gone from the trees, my neighbors have a clear view of this side of the house."

"What's on the other side of the house?"

Grant noted the eagerness in her voice and the way she started toward the other rooms without concern for what she'd find behind the closed doors.

"My bedroom."

She abruptly halted, pivoting around. Reflexively, she caught herself. "You wouldn't want guests running through your bedroom."

"You didn't mention guests when you sold me the spa," he said. "Do you entertain in your spa?"

His question seemed completely innocent, but his eyes were studying her intensely again. "No. I just thought since you're a bachelor that—"

"Stop pigeonholing me. You'd be insulted if I made a similar assumption because you're a divorcee." Her preconceived notions about men in general and himself in particular irked him. Grant raked his hand through his hair in exasperation. "You're nervous as hell about going into my bedroom. Do you think I'm going to start foaming at the mouth and pounce on you?"

Jessica recoiled defensively. "You haven't exactly made a secret of the fact that you wouldn't mind—"

"Wouldn't mind," Grant mimicked caustically. "Is that a polite euphemism for want? Say what you mean."

"All right. You want me. Of course I'm nervous about going into your bedroom. I won't—"

"Lady, don't tell me what you won't do. Less than two hours ago you would have come to me willingly."

100

He raised his hand to keep her from interrupting. "I haven't lived the life of a monk, but I damned sure don't keep a different woman in every bedroom in the house, either. You've confused me with Nicky. He's the skirt-chaser, not me. He's the one who—"

"Stop! Shut up!" Jessica covered her mouth with the back of her hand.

"No, I won't. I know you well enough to know that dishonesty and infidelity sicken you. Me, too." He reached into his pocket and tossed her keys toward her. "That's the unvarnished truth—take it or leave it."

Jessica stooped and picked up the keys. It took every ounce of her breeding and upbringing to keep from hurling them into his face. Through stiff lips she said, "Thank you for dinner and your help, Mr. McDougal. I'll see myself to the door."

CHAPTER SEVEN

The next morning at the shop, Jessica eyed a bulky cardboard box that contained an expensive pool filter. If it didn't cost so darned much, I'd have it delivered to him, she thought. It should just about fit his big mouth!

Unfortunately, Plantation Pools couldn't afford grand gestures.

After spending the night angry and frustrated, she'd hauled herself out of bed at dawn and taken a long, hard look in the mirror. She began to hear not what McDougal had said but what he hadn't said.

She wasn't the only one who'd been flustered when the bedroom was mentioned. Given the chance to have an instant replay, she wondered what he would have done if she'd kept walking in a straight line into his bedroom.

Could he have kept the teasing lightness in his voice? Would the intense directness of his eyes have met hers across the width of his bed? Would want have changed to uncontrollable need?

Yes, indeed, if her reaction had been different, Grand McDougal would have had to face a few truths himself. He'd sandblasted her with anger, but he could have pointed the nozzle in his own direction.

He'd only used Nicky as an excuse to pick a fight. What really bothered him was also what kept him interested: her being a lady. He'd probably call sleeping together "having sex," she mused. But whether they used her polite euphemism or his blunt term, they both knew that she was too much of a lady to become intimate without love.

That's what scared him.

It scared her, too.

Neither of them had been looking for love. She'd avoided it. He'd been too busy building dream houses to find it.

But there love was, staring both of them in the face, daring them to ignore its symptoms. Soulmates, she decided, remembering that he seemed to be able to read her mind. Two people as different as hydrogen and oxygen, and yet they combined to make necessary, life-sustaining water.

Jessica nudged the box with her toe, then gave it a swift kick.

"Wrong filter delivered?" Louise asked from the door to the storage room.

"Wrong destination scheduled. I know a man who's in dire need of it."

"We could order another one and have it shipped express," Louise suggested.

A tight smile curved Jessica's lips. "He's a contractor. He muddied the waters. Let him provide his own filter."

Ever helpful, Louise said, "I could call him and tell him which company gives the biggest discount."

"Or I could call," Jessica responded thoughtfully.

Louise laughed. "That's my job. Could there be

103

some other reason for you wanting to call?" Her head turned toward the display room. "Speaking of my job, the phone is ringing. It's Rose McDougal, probably. Anytime you aren't in her backyard, she's on the phone. Are you here or heading out the back door?"

"I'll take it if it's for me."

Jessica followed Louise to her desk.

"Good morning, Plantation Pools. We design, install, and attend the first pool party," Louise said, cheerfully repeating the company slogan. "Yes, Mrs. McDougal. She's here."

Jessica watched Louise's eyes roll to the ceiling as she took the receiver from her hand.

"Yes, Rose. What's the problem?"

"Hello, dear. It's nothing earthshaking like killing the oak tree. I'm calling about those nice men you sent over here to weave an iron basket in the bottom of the pool."

Jessica chuckled at Rose's description of the ironworkers who were installing the reinforcement rods. "Yes?"

"They want to know what they should do with the black plastic covering the hole."

"Tell them to fold it and roll it as neatly as possible. I'll have one of my men stop by later to pick it up and take it to Grant."

"I could call him and ask him to pick it up, if you're going to be here. Have you had breakfast?" Jessica tried to get a word in edgewise, to tell her not to bother Grant, but before she could speak, Rose said, "Grant used to eat a big breakfast when he was a boy. And take a chewy vitamin. He won't admit it, but I think he skips breakfast. That makes him as cross as a grouchy, old bear. Feed him two eggs, a glass of orange juice, and a couple of slices of bacon, and he's as mild-mannered as Clark Kent. You remember Clark Kent, don't you dear?"

Jessica opened her mouth to answer but there was no stopping Rose.

"Superman! Wouldn't it be wonderful to have your own Superman? Of course, I know since I'm Grant's mother that I'm prejudiced, but I bet Grant would be faster than a speeding bullet if he built this pool. For three years I badgered him to build one. He wouldn't. 'You're as stubborn as a mule,' I told him. It's no wonder he isn't married."

"Mrs. McDougal—" Rose McDougal had mastered what Jessica's dad had called the pool-sweep technique. Rose's prattling was like a pool vacuum skimming the bottom of a pool in a dizzy, erratic path. Just as the vacuum's whips stirred up the bottom and the head snarfed up the little pieces of debris until the pool was perfectly clean, Jessica knew Rose was stirring up side issues, making the water cloudy. Before long, the water would be crystal clear, and Rose would have pushed Jessica into the deep end, without water wings.

"Rose, dear. All my dearest friends call me Rose. By the way, did you notice the roses blooming in the courtyard? Pink Passion. Isn't it simply awful the way advertisers use s-e-x to sell products? Just the other day, when I was at the grocery store, I smelled this lovely fragrance the check-out clerk was wearing. Well, I won't tell you what she called it. My goodness, I couldn't get that word to pass through my lips. Which reminds me, all of your workers are certainly well mannered."

"Thank you, but—"

"You've probably noticed how well-mannered Grant is. Oh, I know, he's tactless sometimes and says things he doesn't really mean. Take for instance late last night, when I called him to see if—well, never mind why I called."

Jessica's ears perked up. The water was getting clearer. Automatically, she took a deep breath. She could almost feel Rose's hand on her back, ready for the big push.

"My son told me to mind my own business. Can you imagine that? You'd think I was pestering him into doing something he didn't want to do!"

"What's that, Rose?" Jessica quietly asked.

"Why, my dear, to make certain you attend the little get-together Saturday night."

"What get-together?" Jessica asked, increasingly wary. She wouldn't put it past Rose to arrange an impromptu party just to further her matchmaking efforts.

"Didn't you get an invitation in the mail? When I was talking to Grant's persnickity secretary, she said she was too busy to chat because she was addressing invitations. I made certain your company's name was on the list."

"Rose, exactly what kind of party is this?"

"A party the investors of the new hotel complex are having for potential subcontractors. Didn't you get your invitation?" Rose grinned as she stirred the hornet's nest. "Of course, I wouldn't blame you for not accepting his invitation considering . . . everything."

"Everything?"

"Well, I'm certain you aren't happy with Grant for

106

being rude to me." Rose rolled her tongue in her cheek. Her Kentucky drawl broadened. "Now, I know how loyal you are, but I'm used to dealing with my son's snippiness. I'd just hate it if you lost your chance at that commercial contract just because I'm upset with Grant. You will accept, won't you?"

Jessica braced herself against the desk. Push was coming to shove. "Is Grant's company, North American Contractors, one of the investors?"

"I don't know about money matters, Jessica. You can ask him when you're both here for breakfast!"

Jessica admired Rose's technique of getting her own way, but mentally she was flailing her arms to keep from sinking to the bottom of the pool. No doubt Rose would have Grant jumping in to save her.

But Rose had made one tactical error. Jessica was an expert swimmer. All she had to do was kick up off the bottom of the pool and swim to the side.

First the kick. "I'm scheduled to be at the Herman pool to supervise the tile and coping installation in fifteen minutes." And the freestyle stroke. "I'll decide about the investors' get-together when I've received the invitation."

"But, Jessica—"

"Got to swim—er, run. See you later." Before Rose could make another figurative sweep around the pool, Jessica had hung up the phone. "Whew!"

Louise laughed. "Water-Devil Rose is what I've nicknamed her. You're sucked up into the spout before you see the water rippling!" She put her hand on the phone. "You'd better scat before she has time to call back."

"Right!" Jessica agreed. She wiped her damp hands

on the side of her jumpsuit as she dodged through stacks of boxes, hurrying toward the back entrance. As she closed the door, she heard the phone ring.

She drove to the Herman house, west of the Ashley, thinking about the investors' party. Grant had been noncommittal about Plantation Pools getting the job. Worse, he'd told her that out-of-town contractors were horning in on her territory. And he'd also pointed out how steamlined her competitors' operations were.

Darn it, she needed this commercial pool contract!

Plantation Pools' past reputation for digging ponds instead of pools haunted her. She'd turned the company around from its downhill course by completing those contracts. Slowly but surely, prospective customers were beginning to trust her company again.

Aside from the bothersome accidents at the McDougal job site, she could proudly point to the efficiency of her operation at the other three pools presently under construction. Every week since March, she'd brought a bottle of champagne to mark the completion of another pool: finished on schedule.

She'd juggled subcontractors' schedules with ease. The right crews were at the right job site, on time, and fully equipped. Within an hour of one crew leaving, another was there. If they were late, she pitched in and started the work herself. Personally supervising the work kept her hopping from job to job, but that couldn't be helped.

What flaw had Grant found?

What could be more efficient?

"Efficiency be damned," she muttered in an uncharacteristic slip of the tongue, then she corrected, "darned. Money is the bottom line. The low bidder will get the job."

She felt certain that no out-of-town company could match her price. Food and lodging had to be figured into their costs. Being local, with local suppliers, her bid should at least be in the running. It must, or she wouldn't be getting an invitation.

The thought that McDougal had added her name to the list for reasons other than business didn't cross her mind.

While Jessica gnawed at her lip, Grant was biting nails.

"Mother, stop playing cupid," he gritted into the phone, lowering his voice to keep the man across his desk from overhearing the conversation. "And stop the runaround. It won't work with me."

"You don't have to jump down my throat. See what happens when you don't eat breakfast? Jessica was grouchy when I talked to her, too. She did perk up when I mentioned your invitation."

Grant muffled a groan with his hand. "That's business, Mother, not a social occasion."

"From what your secretary says, there will be enough people there for a small ball."

"Contractors don't have balls."

Rose paused dramatically. Her eyebrow arched. "Well, dear, if you say so."

Unable to help himself, Grant grinned. His mother might serve lemonade and tea cakes, but sometimes her humor was decidedly earthy. He glanced across the desk and noted the small grin Craig Newsom couldn't conceal.

"How's the pool coming along?" Grant asked. "Any accidents?"

"Not yet."

"Let's hope not. The only thing they haven't wrecked is the house."

"You're exaggerating, Grant. Jessica's men finished eating your breakfast and they're back at work."

Grant leaned forward in his leather chair. "You're feeding them when they're supposed to be working?"

"You didn't want the food wasted, did you? Think about those poor children in Africa. Don't you dare tell me to pack it up and send it to them," she warned, slightly indignant. "Those nice men raved about my eggs Benedict so much that I'm going to fix lunch for them."

"You're slowing down their work, Mother."

"They'll work faster after a nice dinner of southern fried chicken with mashed potatoes and gravy, and fresh pecan pie for dessert. You should see the pitiful size of their lunch sacks. I couldn't let them do all that hard work on peanut butter and jelly sandwiches, could I?"

"Thirty days," he reminded. "On day thirty-one, if it isn't completed, my men will fill in the hole with dirt."

"Well, maybe I won't fix the pecan pie," Rose conceded.

"That's good of you. I'm certain Jessica will appreciate your thoughtfulness. 'Bye."

Grant apologized to Craig, an electrical subcontractor who'd worked for Grant since the early days of Northern Contractors of America, for the interruption.

"Sounds like Rose is enjoying the pool before it's completed," Craig commented, grinning. "Remember when I had my men string the wires for the outside lighting?"

"Yeah. A two-hour job took two days."

"Your mother talked the electricians' ears off while she poked food into their mouths. Whoever contracted to build a pool in thirty days didn't know her."

Grant flipped the corner of a stack of blueprints. Craig, a Charlestonian, could fill in a lot of blanks regarding Jessica. "Plantation Pools."

"Ah, the Hayes company."

"You know the family?"

"Sure. Jessica's old Charleston." Craig's forefinger tapped his lips as he recalled Jessica to mind. "Lives out on what used to be the family rice plantation. Graduated from Ashley Hall while I was at the Citadel. She rocked the town back onto its button-toed shoes when she divorced the cad she was married to and started running the family business. You know, I haven't thought about Jess in years. We're third cousins by marriage. Kissin' cousins, you might say." A speculative smile curved his lips.

"Wipe the leer off your face," Grant said, regretting having brought up Jessica's name. "Have you forgotten a certain Georgia peach named Nancy who you've had the hots for?"

"Nancy who?"

"Nancy Who Robertson. That's Nancy Who," Grant snorted. "You've been chasing her for six months. How could you forget?"

"Jessica Hayes is the kind of lady who could make

111

me forget the difference between positive and negative currents," Craig quipped.

"That could get you killed."

Craig grinned. "It'd be worth it."

"Plantation Pools submitted a bid on the hotel complex pool," Grant said, deciding he'd be safer discussing business. Listening to Craig moon about Jessica disturbed him. How many other men got the same dreamy look in their eyes when they heard her name? He didn't know, and he didn't want to know.

"Great! She ought to be over her husband by now. Maybe"—Craig rubbed his chin thoughtfully, unaware of the muscle twitching on his boss's hard jaw— "maybe, if she's going commercial, she'll let me wire her pools—or anything else she needs to have wired."

Jealousy hammered through Grant with the force of an electric nail driver. "Sounds to me like you're overestimating your own voltage. You aren't wired for two twenties."

Craig gave a particularly male chuckle in response. "She'd be a live wire all right," he admitted. "What are her chances of getting the job?"

"Almost nil. Indigo Pools out of Texas has the lowest bid and the best reputation."

"I thought you'd convinced the other investors that using local contractors, who'd be here if something went wrong a year after completion, was the best policy."

"Recommended," Grant corrected, "not convinced. That's why Jim Barnes and Bill Cooper insisted on meeting the prospective contractors face to face socially."

"To size us up before they give the contracts? In

112

that case, Plantation Pools is a cinch to get the contract. Jim and Bill will take one look at Jessica's hip-length blond hair and double the number of pools they've planned. Hell, they'll probably add hot spas to every suite of rooms."

"Don't kid yourself, Craig. Those men may mix business and pleasure by having an informal dinner dance, but when it comes to plunking down hard cash, they'll award the contract to people who can make them the most money." Grant rose and crossed to the drafting table, where a thick pile of architectural drawings was spread. "Any more questions about the underground electrical cables?"

"No, but I have one about Jessica. Do you plan on escorting her Saturday night? It might help her chances if she showed up with you."

"My, what big ears you have," Grant said, glancing from Craig's face to the phone. "Mother made the same suggestion."

Craig stood up from the chair, crossed to Grant, and gave him a hearty slap on the shoulders. A spark of amusement lit his eyes. "Southerners have to stick together when there's a coldhearted Yankee in our midst."

"General Lee may have surrendered at Appomattox, but the South didn't." Grant gave Craig a shrewd look as he shook his hand. "I'll see you Saturday night."

After Craig left his office, Grant sorted through the blueprints until he found the plumbing diagram. His finger moved from one king-size bathroom to the next. "Stephanie," he roared, not bothering to use the inter-

113

com, "bring in the plumbing bids and the pool bids from the files."

Minutes later, Grant had scanned the sheets his secretary had brought in. A satisfied smile curved his lips. He punched the intercom and told Stephanie to place a call to Jessica Hayes at Plantation Pools. His fingers steepled as he leaned back in his chair and waited.

"Mr. McDougal, Plantation Pools is on line three."

Grant picked up the phone. "Jessica?"

"No, sir. Jessica isn't available. This is Louise, her assistant. May I take a message?"

"Grant McDougal. Tell Jessica I've decided about the spa we discussed. I'd like a bid for sixteen of them."

"Sixteen?" Louise squawked, uncertain she'd heard him correctly. She'd instantly connected Rose McDougal with Grant McDougal. But what would any sane person do with a swimming pool and sixteen spas? "You're certain?"

"Sixteen," Grant confirmed. Not taking any chances, he added, "Tell her I'll pick her up Saturday evening at seven. We'll discuss the specifics then."

"I'm afraid I can't—" Louise stopped talking when she heard the line disconnected. "Oh, Lordy," she whispered, shaking her head as she hung up the phone. She had a sneaking suspicion that Jessica was in over her head. Way over her head.

CHAPTER EIGHT

"Sixteen spas? Has he gone bonkers!" Jessica's voice rose in disbelief. The grand gesture she'd considered sending him hardly compared to his. What was he going to do—open a geisha club on Kiawah? This had to be a joke! "Well, McDougal, it fell flatter than a fritter. I'm not going to waste my time preparing a bid."

She sorted through the remainder of the mail Louise had left. On a small envelope, a note penned in Louise's scrawl read, "Mr. McDougal will pick you up at seven."

"What!" She ripped the envelope open and read aloud, "As a prospective subcontractor, you are cordially invited to attend a dinner dance sponsored by The Investors Group, Limited. Bring a guest." Her eyes scanned the date, time, and place. "Rose must have put an armlock on her son. Mouthlock," she corrected, remembering that she must have looked like a fish gasping for air when she tried to get a word in edgewise on the phone.

She tapped the corner of the invitation against her lip. Command performance, eh, McDougal? Between job sites, she'd been trying to figure out a way to graciously apologize for her hasty departure the previous evening. She'd even stopped at a card shop to get a bread-and-butter note to send him, to thank him for dinner. Nobody, including Grant McDougal, could fault her good manners.

McDougal must have been similarly occupied, she mused with a grin. She liked the thought of McDougal plotting their next skirmish. Still, telling her secretary he'd be her escort—at his mother's prompting—made the short hairs at her nape bristle.

"High-handed," she said, disgruntled, disliking the thought of anyone's mother fixing her up with a date. Rose had engineered the whole setup from the beginning, from pool to party.

The idea of McDougal as a mama's boy fleetingly crossed her mind. Just as fleetingly it vanished into thin air. Rose and Grant were strong-willed individuals. As an observer of their ongoing tug-of-war, Jessica could give each of them points but neither a victory. She just had to avoid being the one who ended up in the mud puddle.

She broke one of her cardinal rules: she looked up the number of Northern Contractors of America in the directory, picked up the phone, and dialed his office. He wasn't the only person who could be high-handed. She'd teach him a lesson in manners!

"McDougal speaking," he said after the third ring.

"Hayes here. I called about your gracious invitation to the dinner dance Saturday night," she said in saccharine-smooth tones.

Grant straightened, undeceived by the mildness of her voice. Jessica was a lady, but he knew she wouldn't take kindly to his scheduling himself into her

116

social calendar. A strong diversionary tactic was necessary to conceal his main attack.

"Fifteen of those spas are to be installed in the hotel complex. The plumbing contractors who bid for the job must have thought the pool builder would install them, and vice versa. One spa is for my house at Kiawah." Grant charged ahead nonstop. He hadn't been raised by Rose without learning something. "I'll expect my spa to be installed on the porch off the master suite first."

"McDougal—" Jessica sputtered, assimilating the information and gasping for air.

"The ones in the hotel complex should be beige, to match the carpeting. You'll have to get together with the carpet contractor and the interior decorator at the dinner. Black is fine with me. Speaking of black, the investors are wearing summer tuxedos to the dinner. Since we'll be attending together, you'll want to wear something dressy. I figured you'd wear your hair up, so I took the liberty of ordering your flowers set in a hair comb. Southern magnolias."

Grant chuckled, inhaling deeply for the final coup de grâce. "I'm looking forward to Saturday night. I'll be thinking of you while I'm in Richmond the rest of the week. Oh, incidentally, your ironworkers won't be finished tomorrow."

"What!"

"You heard me. Rose fed them breakfast and lunch. In this heat, heavy meals slow down a worker's pace. Better keep an eye on them while I'm in Richmond looking over a refurbishing project in the historic district. Grant took Richmond in 1864. Looks like his descendant is going to have a chance to rebuild, huh?

117

You might want to ask Rose about her infamous relatives. I've missed you, lady. 'Bye."

"Wait a minute! Wait! Don't you dare"—she heard the line being disconnected—"hang up!"

She banged the telephone down. "Rose Water-Devil McDougal and her son, Tornado Mouth! You aren't going to get away with this!" she muttered, dialing the same number. "Busy signal!"

Overcome with an urge to throw things, stomp, and scream, Jessica jumped to her feet and paced. Darn it! At least Rose had given her a chance to kick off the bottom and paddle away. Grant had pulled her into his whirlwind and left her sucking air like an unprimed pump!

"You aren't going to get away with this," she stormed, dialing for a third time. "Grant took Richmond, not Charleston!"

"North American Contractors. The office has closed for the day. Our hours are between—"

"A recording! Blast you, Grant McDougal! Sandblast you!" she added for good measure. For two cents she'd leave a message on the recorder that would scald his ears. Something outrageous! Her eyes narrowed. Something very unladylike!

As Jessica fumed, Grant leaned back in his chair, feeling supremely satisfied with himself. Not even his mother, with her faster-than-the-speed-of-sound tongue, could have done better. But unlike Rose's shotgun pattern, which spread all over the place, he'd taken aim and delivered his bits of information with the speed and precision of a machine gun.

"And now, sweet Jessica, it's time to retreat, regroup, and conquer!" he said, rising to his feet, marching to the door.

As he crossed through his secretary's office, he heard the recorded message on his answering machine. "Stephanie must have left the speaker on," he muttered, wondering why. He considered picking up the phone, but one quick glance at his watch told him that he'd miss his flight if he got into a long-winded discussion with one of his foremen.

"Ah'm calling for Grant McDougal," a breathy, husky voice said. Sex appeal dripped from every elongated vowel.

Grant barely recognized Jessica's voice.

"Would ya'll tell Yankee Doodle that ah just don't know if little ol' me can find anything to wear for the party, but ah'll have the spa hot and bubbly, just waitin' for his magnolias. Ya'll come now, ya hear?"

"Hell's belles!" Grant said astounded, giving his favorite polite curse words a new meaning.

A vivid mental picture of Jessica nude in the spa with magnolias floating on the surface of the steaming water made him very much aware of his manhood. His imagination went wild until he tossed his head back and roared with laughter. After a beckoning invitation like that, he'd have to crawl to the company airplane. She'd Yankee Doodled his dandy!

He gave a mock salute toward the recorder, then rewound it and erased the message. "Direct hit, lady, right below the belt."

Both of them smiled as they planned their next attack.

By lunchtime the following Saturday, Jessica's schedule on the McDougal pool was four days behind. She couldn't afford those four days any more than she could afford the expensive outfit she'd bought for the dinner dance. And if she didn't get the plumber and the electrician out of Rose's kitchen, she'd miss her thirty-day deadline for certain. Every man on the crew must have gained ten pounds!

Unwilling to embarrass Rose by making a scene in front of the men, she'd paced back and forth outside until she heard the screen door bang, signaling the departure of the crew from the back porch.

Ready to grab the Water Devil by the tail, she mounted the steps.

"Jessica dear," Rose greeted, warmly hugging her as Jessica strode into the kitchen. "We just finished having a little bit to eat. Won't you have some chicken and dumplings?"

"No, Rose," Jessica answered firmly as she surveyed the near-empty platters and bowls. "No chicken and dumplings. No Waldorf salad. No homemade biscuits. Nothing."

Rose smiled. "You're too excited about tonight to eat, aren't you? I remember the first dance Grant's father took me to when I was sixteen. Hoops and laces had made a comeback. Mother made this darling gown with layer upon layer of frothy yellow nylon net. A wide moss-green satin ribbon slashed across from my shoulder to my waist. Grant's father said he'd never seen me look more beautiful. It was that night when he first proposed. Of course, I was too young for marriage." She paused and gave Jessica a look that said, "But you aren't."

"Rose, *please!*" She held up both hands to stop the reminiscing. "No more culinary feasts for the men. I'm supposed to be at home getting ready for the dinner tonight, and I'm here shooing the crew that I've had to pay double time away from your table. I'll never get this pool finished! Not in thirty days, not in thirty years!"

"Don't worry about the deadline," Rose dismissed airily, collecting dishes from the table and taking them to the sink. "I'm not. I'm enjoying myself immensely. I haven't had this much fun since the electricians were here installing the floodlights."

Silently, Jessica moaned at Rose's utter obtuseness about the ripple effect of delaying schedules. One delayed schedule affected all her work. The men outside, who were loudly burping, were days late getting to the other pools. She'd spent the week running helter-skelter, explaining to other homeowners why their pools were being delayed. But Rose was lonely. Having a backyard filled with people to visit with and feed was an opportunity that she wasn't about to miss just because of some unimportant deadline. What did Jessica have to do to make Rose understand the problem? There had to be a way to make her stop interfering with the work schedule.

Hands on her temples, Jessica spoke slowly and precisely in an effort to give Rose a clear picture of the consequences of providing the workers with a daily pig-out.

"On day thirty-one, Grant has threatened to fill the

hole with dirt. You won't have a swimming pool, and I won't collect."

Rose flashed Jessica a cheeky grin. "I'll write you a check. Do you need one now?"

"How high will this check bounce?" Jessica gamely asked, remembering that Grant had had to switch funds to cover the first one.

"Grant manages my money, but it is *my* money. Don't worry, dear. I'll take care of Grant. I always have. He may be a little quarrelsome to begin with, but he wants to see me happy." Rose leaned toward Jessica and patted her hand. "And that's what I want for him. To see him happy."

"Believe me, he isn't going to be rollicking with laughter when he comes back and sees how little has been accomplished since he went to Richmond," Jessica warned.

"Exactly," Rose said, as if Jessica had proven her point. "He always comes back from his out-of-town trips all hot and bothered. That's why he needs you."

"You've confused the order of events. First he'll come back to Charleston, and then when he sees an empty hole in the backyard, that's when he'll get all hot and bothered. The only thing he'll need me for is to fill the space below the knot in the hangman's noose after he tosses it over the branch of an oak tree."

Rose chuckled and made a dismissive motion with one hand. "Grant didn't hang southern belles in 1865, regardless of what they did. My Grant won't hang you, either."

Jessica had the same sinking sensation in the pit of her stomach that Robert E. Lee must have had when he was in the wilderness, battling against the odds, knowing that surrender was in the immediate future. There was no conquering Rose McDougal. She was prepared for every eventuality.

"I'm willing to compromise," Rose offered, scraping the last morsels from a plate into the garbage disposal.

Jessica sighed. "Anything."

"I won't feed the men their afternoon snack, if you'll go home and get yourself prettied up for tonight."

Gracefully, if not graciously, Jessica groaned as she headed toward the door. "You win."

After Rose heard the screen door close, she grinned from ear to ear. "I always do, dear, I always do." Her eyes sparkled with mirth as she added, "But only when both sides want me to win."

The ride home failed to soothe Jessica's nerves. Grant might not hang her, but she had a sneaking suspicion that after he received her message on the office recorder, he'd have another item to be hot and bothered over. For the thousandth time she chastized herself for the message, but at least she'd been clever enough not to leave her name. Only Grant would know.

Jessica turned the air-conditioning vent on the dashboard directly onto her heated face. McDougal wasn't the only one who was hot and bothered, she thought dryly. Wedged between her hectic daytimes had been several long, lonely nights in a double bed that had grown to the proportions of a king-size bed.

Each morning she awakened with a queasy ache at the juncture of her thighs, as if she'd just been passionately kissed but then left lingering in frustration. At

123

times she'd caught herself remembering the feel of Grant's lips and hands.

The memories puzzled her. After Nicky had deserted her, she had been so concerned about picking up the pieces of her business that she hadn't missed him in a physical sense. The more she thought about it, the more she realized that in the last few months before their separation they hadn't shared even the intimacy of a good-night kiss. She hadn't missed the kisses, then nor now. Not from Nicky.

But she couldn't ignore her heart thudding heavily in her chest when she thought about Grant's slow, mind-drugging kisses. The way his large hands had caressed her sent shivers down her spine. It had been a long, long time since she'd wanted any man's attention. Perhaps that explained the acute, gnawing hunger she felt when she thought of Grant.

She'd promised herself over and over again to be as plain-spoken with Grant as he'd been with her. The silver lamé gown hanging in her closet was a testimony to her intent to be bold and daring, forthright and honest.

"Sexy as all get out," the saleswoman had said as Jessica twirled in front of the mirror.

Garbed in her jumpsuit, Grant had still considered her to be a lady. She wondered if *lady* and *sexy* equaled *woman*. Tonight, she wanted to be all woman. Soft. Seductive. Feminine. Wild. She wanted to hear Grant's back molars grinding as he anticipated unhooking the single hook over the long expanse of bare back that held the gown in place.

The gown was deceptively simple with its high neck and inch-wide rhinestone collar. She'd be deceptively simple, too. Only the long slit up the side, which exposed a flash of silky thigh as she walked, hinted at the sensuality hidden beneath. In the back—what there was of it—the flimsy fabric dipped into a low teardrop. It snugly fit the curve of her body but left her back bare inches below her waist.

As she drove, she began removing the rubber bands from the rows of small braids in her hair. She knew that brushing it would send it, curling wickedly, cascading down her back. At first she'd considered wearing it piled high on her head with Grant's magnolias artfully woven into a mass of curls. But she decided to part her hair on the side, letting the flowered combs hold one side back from her face and letting the other side flow free. Her hair would swish back and forth and give tantalizing glimpses of her back. A seductive whisper that would be heard louder than a gun-shot was the effect she wanted.

Several hours later, groomed and perfumed, Jessica answered the door. She felt as if she were on the wrong end of the pistol. She instantly learned the meaning of the phrase *dressed to kill*. Grant McDougal—with the white jacket of his summer tuxedo contrasting with his deep tan, with a pale blue cummerbund that matched the intense color of his eyes, and with a long stripe of satin accenting his masculine legs—was devastating.

"I got your message," Grant said in a voice gentler than the warm summer breeze lightly blowing off the marshland. He straightened from leaning against the doorjamb and brushed his lips across hers. "I'm looking forward to seeing your spa."

"S-s-spa?" Her mind went totally blank as she attempted to savor the polite kiss by licking her lower lip. She blinked twice, three times, to orient herself. Ladies swooned; Jessica felt faint. Remembering her manners, she said, "Won't you come in?"

Grant saw the residue of moisture clinging to the lips she'd just licked; he saw her mouth move, but the words didn't register. The message she'd left on the tape recorder hadn't prepared him for this battle. She was a vision of loveliness and sensuality. Lordy, Lordy, he thought, all I want to do is surrender unconditionally—and be revived in the spa!

"I beg your pardon?" they both said in unison, then chuckled at their inappropriate remark. "You look beautiful." Again, in unison.

Every clever, witty word that Jessica planned to say was stuck behind the lump in her throat. To her own ears her voice sounded strangled as she said, "First we think alike, now we're saying the same things. Is that a good omen for the evening?"

"Definitely," Grant said.

"Won't you come in for a drink? I fixed mint juleps." A teasing light brightened her eyes. She raised her hand to the flowers in her hair. "Mint juleps go with magnolias, don't they?"

"Mmm-hm. Also moonlight, starry skies, and steamy spas. I think I'll take a raincheck till later." He turned toward the driveway. "Your chariot awaits you, lady."

Jessica's eyes followed his hand. They widened as they came to rest on a long, low Lincoln limousine. "A limo? I've never ridden in one, but I've always wanted to."

"I thought it befit the occasion. The closest thing I could find to a horse-drawn carriage was the tourist

126

variety down in the Market area." He rubbed his cleanly shaven chin thoughtfully. "I made the wrong choice."

Hooking her hand through the crook of his elbow, Jessica brushed against him and smiled knowingly. "It'd take hours to get to Charleston in a carriage."

"Hours well spent," Grant replied. He couldn't resist touching the cloud of hair held in suspension by the magnolias he'd had delivered. Her fragrance combined with the flowers to make a heady scent. "I would have had you alone for long, lovely hours, rather than spent them sharing you with a batch of hungry wolves at the Marriott."

"I trust you'll keep the wolves at bay?" She hoped her smile told him that she couldn't think of a lovelier way to spend the next few hours, either. "Let me get my evening purse."

Jessica turned, took four steps, and heard a low, admiring wolf whistle.

"Like it?" she asked, giving him a sexy wink.

"Oh, lady, you're asking for trouble!"

She picked up her beaded evening bag and sauntered toward Grant. She watched his eyes appreciatively move to the flowing slit that gave shimmering glances of her long legs. Something between a gasp, a hiss, and a low moan came between his lips. Lazily she reached up to trace the firmness of his clenched jaw with a manicured nail.

"Ah do hope trouble is your middle name." With a husky laugh, she preceded him down the front steps. "Coming?"

"Lord help me," he muttered to himself. "Uh, Jessica, before we leave—"

"Yes?" Her voice dipped as she stretched the vowel for all it was worth.

Grant took one of her hands in his, then rested his other hand at the back of her bare waist. "Do you have *anything* on under that confection?"

"Of course," she replied loftily. She felt his hand move higher across her back. His eyes drifted to the the slight cling of the fabric over her bottom.

"What?"

Jessica raised one lightly penciled eyebrow and whispered, "Your imagination and my dignity."

CHAPTER NINE

The sweeping glance, the intense blueness of Grant's eyes as they lingered on her gave Jessica the confidence she needed to mingle with the powerful investors. They held the fate of Plantation Pools in their hands. She'd survive without the contract, but her company wouldn't expand beyond Charleston's limited horizons.

After everyone had partaken of the delicious buffet, the tables had been cleared, and they had moved to the perimeter of the room. While the room was being cleared, Jessica excused herself to freshen her lipstick. By the time she returned, a band was set up, playing a bouncy popular tune.

Her eyes scanned the room. A small smile played at her mouth as she noticed three distinct groupings. To the right of the dance floor, the Charlestonians had closed ranks. To the left, out-of-town contractors gave the appearance of being jovial, but she noticed the speculative glances being shot across the room. In the center, between the two groups, the small gathering of investors, including Grant, were seated. She noticed that occasionally members of each group strayed across the invisible lines.

Jessica jumped, startled, when someone behind her touched her bare shoulder.

"Sorry," Craig said, "I didn't mean to scare you. What are you doing standing on the sidelines?"

She and Craig had exchanged polite greetings earlier. "I'm watching the action." She tilted her head to the far side of the room. "The way our confederates are shooting glares across the room, I think Fort Sumter is about to be fired upon."

Craig laughed. "I've been on the receiving end of a few of their glances, too." He shivered as if a cold breeze had just gusted through the doorway. Dryly he said, "Instead of Carolina building code books, I think they brought a copy of *Uncle Tom's Cabin.*"

"Where's your southern hospitality?" she asked with a challenging look. "Come on!"

Jessica took his arm and strolled in a northerly direction. Her warm, welcoming smile as she introduced herself and Craig disarmed the hostile coolness within seconds.

Contracts, employees, and building problems provided a neutral ground for conversation. Once the ice had been broken, several acquaintances of Jessica's joined them. Humorous stories were swapped back and forth. Where there had been a strained silence, now there was laughter. The group slowly expanded.

A short distance away, Grant stood in the rapidly disintegrating knot of investors. They, too, were drawn to the warmth of Jessica's fire. She'd become the unofficial hostess, the belle of the ball.

Bill Cooper held her hand in greeting for seconds longer than necessary, Grant thought. With gritted teeth, he smiled as Jessica caught his eye before accepting Bill's invitation to dance. He knew that the crystal blue clarity of her eyes would reflect the light as she lifted her head and smiled her acceptance at Bill.

Jessica nodded in his direction. Bill twirled her around, laughed, and loosened his grip at the back of her waist. Grant was considering stepping in when he realized that Craig and Nancy were standing beside him.

"Don't let us stop you," Craig said, following Grant's intense stare. A small, knowing smile lifted the corner of his mouth. "You can't blame Cooper for trying. He's a widower, I've heard."

"And old enough to be her father," Nancy commented. She squeezed Craig's arm between hers and the full softness of her breast. "See what happens when a man takes a woman for *grant*ed?"

Both men chuckled at her low-keyed pun, which used Grant's name and poked fun at Craig at the same time.

"You can't fault a man for looking," Craig retorted, dropping a swift kiss on Nancy's forehead. "I'm not dead."

"Yet," Nancy quipped.

Grant listened to the give-and-take between Craig and his girl friend, but his eyes remained on Jessica. As Bill masterfully swirled her in several fast steps, he heard her bubble of laughter. This is too much, he thought, unable to resist any longer. The last strains of the song echoed in his ears as he turned to Craig and Nancy. "Would you excuse me?"

Craig's satisfied smile and Nancy's kitten-who'd-just-licked-the-cream-from-her-whiskers grin were the

131

last things Grant saw before he purposely strode onto the dance floor. Over Bill's shoulder, he saw the expectant look in Jessica's eyes. She seemed to be holding her breath in anticipation.

The scent of magnolias engulfed him an instant before he slipped his arm around her waist and pulled her gently toward himself. The narrowed intensity of his eyes challenged the older man. Jessica pressed close to his side.

"Grant! Jessica has been telling me about the pool she's building for Rose," Bill said. "Think I can talk your mother into inviting me to her opening pool party?"

Brightly smiling, although her facial muscles felt stiff, Jessica watched the McDougal twinkle in Grant's eyes as he measured Bill as a suitable match for his mother. "You'll have my personal invitation, if you'll allow me to take Jessica away from you for the next dance."

Bill glanced reluctantly from Jessica to Grant. He shrugged. "Be my guest."

The music started. Jessica slipped her arms around Grant's neck. The tension between the men during their exchange left her feeling splendidly gorgeous. A tingle of awareness skated down her spine as Grant's hands claimed her, drawing her into the cradle of his hips.

"Are you thinking what I think you're thinking?" Jessica inquired, resting her cheek on his satin lapel.

"Rose and Bill?"

Her head rose, lips seeking and finding the warm flesh above his starched collar. "Mmmmm."

Jessica's reply hummed through her lips. It was

both an answer and a tribute to his pleasant masculine smell. Beneath her fingertips she felt his shoulder muscles knot as her breath fanned the pulse point on his throat.

"What I'm thinking doesn't qualify as polite dance floor conversation."

"Mmmmm."

"One more of those sultry 'mmmmm's' " Grant warned, "and my intention to behave like a gentleman is going to go right down the tubes."

Her eyelashes fluttered against his neck like small, fragile butterflies. "I've been practicing in front of the mirror all week." She sighed.

"Practicing what? Seduction?" Grant answered his own question. "Lady, you can't improve on perfection. My libido and my good intentions are brawling for supremacy."

He swayed against her, shifting her into a safer position with his leg between hers. Merely feeling her soft breasts against his chest made him rock hard. He silently cursed his lack of gentlemanly control.

Jessica smiled secretly. It wasn't necessary to be a mind reader to know who was winning. She leaned back in his arms, which resulted in their legs intimately touching. "I've practiced speaking bluntly."

"Don't! For the sake of propriety, not now! One honest word coming from those kissable lips, and I'll be barred from future social functions."

Despite his warning, she was pulled closer. Her low, husky laugh tormented him. His hands made small forays beneath her long swath of hair.

"Silky hair and satiny skin," he breathed close to her ear.

"Hair and skin," she corrected bluntly, enjoying her own refreshing bluntness. "Everybody has them."

His fingers followed the small indentations in the curve of her shoulders. "Now I know why gentlemen used to be required to wear gloves."

"I'd hate gloves. Your hands are warm and strong—like you."

"And why the waltz was banned in Boston." His teeth nibbled the shell of her ear. "Soon, very soon, I'm going to drive you wild, lady."

"Woman, not lady. Ladies are never wild. Haven't you noticed?"

"Noticed what?"

"Tonight I'm—"

"Hush, woman. I know what you are, and it's going to embarrass you when this dance ends if they turn up the lights."

"Mr. McDougal, that's as close as you've been all night to bluntness. I'd begun to think you didn't want me." She let her wealth of hair hide the tiny licks she made along the strong column of his neck. His unique taste exploded on her taste buds, making her want more. "The way I want you."

Grant audibly groaned in his frustration. He slowly led them dancing to the outside door. His hand lazily rested on her hip as he opened the door. In the warm, sultry darkness he watched her eyes flutter open.

"Lady, you've taken every bit of glibness right out of me." His eyes strained to find a secluded spot. "To hell with privacy!"

His mouth claimed hers with all the fiery passion she'd dreamed of. Her lips parted as his tongue branded hers. Her knees felt watery. She wrapped her arms tightly around his waist, holding on for balance, seemingly for dear life.

She met his velvet thrusts with her own. Without speaking, his tongue told her that he wanted to be deep inside her, luxuriating in her honeyed warmth, discovering her secrets. They were soulmates.

His fingers twined in her hair at the base of her neck as he reluctantly ended their kiss. He rocked his brow against hers, as if she could read his mind, divine his thoughts, by touching. His breathing was ragged, too harsh for anything other than her name. "Jessica . . ."

"Not enough," she enticed. The tip of her tongue glossed over the bow of his lip. "Not nearly enough."

"You're one incredibly sexy lady," he murmured, eyes closing, unable to continue, unable to stop her. "In an incredibly public place."

Jessica had long forgotten her reason for attending the dinner. She'd done her duty, made an appearance, socialized. Thoughts of swimming pools had vanished from her mind, but tantalizing thoughts of spas had not.

"Moonlit night. Magnolias. You." She burrowed into the wide cradle of his hips. "Something's missing."

"More kissing?" Grant suggested, his mouth hovering over hers.

"My spa. Warm bubbling water. Summer breezes blowing off the marshes." She paused, testing his desire for honesty. "Sex?"

"Making love?" he said, altering the blunt word with a sweet kiss.

"Decadent sex in the raw." She watched the smol-

135

dering passion in the dark of his eyes change to amusement. Her chin tilted to a cocky angle. "Took me two hours of practice to be able to say that one."

"I believe it. With my eyes closed I painted a picture of water, sky, and ecstasy. Sex is too harsh." Grant tucked a stray lock of hair behind her ear. "It doesn't quite fit the picture."

"McDougal," she chided, "are you telling me you like my romantic version more than your honest-to-the-bare-bone directness?"

In the darkness, Jessica could barely see his head nod. "Reminds me of the time I was eleven or twelve when I told my dad that God had made a mistake by not giving boys X-ray vision. He wasn't a particularly devout man, but he gave me a hard look and said, 'Son, you're the one who's mistaken. How would you like looking at bones and skulls?' I should have remembered that boyhood lesson."

"Our fathers must be kindred spirits. My dad was a classical kind of man. Had he lived a hundred years ago, he would have been called Colonel. He loved the slow, leisurely pace of the South." Jessica smiled, remembering all the times he'd given her good advice and forgetting how he'd pressured her into marriage. "No thirty-day deadlines for him. That wouldn't allow time to inhale the fragrance of azaleas in the spring or feel the salt air blowing off the Atlantic. Sometimes I forget the values he taught me."

Grant tucked her under his arm and turned their backs on the party. With measured steps, his matching hers, they walked toward the parking lot.

"Look!" Jessica stopped and pointed to a shooting star. "Close your eyes and make a wish."

Jessica clamped her eyes shut. *I wish . . . I wish Grant loved me as much as I love him.* She opened her eyes, suddenly overcome with shyness as she glanced at the tall, handsome man beside her—the only man who could grant her wish.

Grant lifted her hand to his mouth and placed a warm kiss in her palm. Then he slowly curled her fingers over it for safe keeping. "Hold on to that wish and the kiss. I'll get your purse and say our goodbyes."

Hugging herself, she kept her hand closed as if she were holding a priceless treasure and strolled toward the limo. From the corner of her eye, she saw the driver jogging toward the car. She slowed her pace to give him time to reach the car first.

He touched the brim of his cap and asked, "Ma'am, will Mr. McDougal be joining you, or should I drive you home and come back for him?"

"He'll be joining me," Jessica answered with a smug smile. Casting a glance over her shoulder, she saw Grant hurrying toward the car. Secure with that knowledge, she settled into the plush backseat and waited.

"C'mere," Grant invited once he'd murmured instructions to the driver and climbed into the backseat. "There's something to be said for not having to keep my eyes on the road."

"Or your hands on the wheel," she agreed.

Without realizing exactly how Grant managed it, she found herself across his lap, her arm around his shoulder.

"Okay?" he asked as he leaned forward and closed

the tinted glass between the driver's seat and the back-seat. "I'm fresh out of newspapers."

Rubbing her finger along his curved mouth, she said, "And I'm fresh out of worrying about it."

He parted his lips, gently sucking on the tip of her finger. "Slow and easy," he whispered.

"Not too slow." Jessica unclipped his bow tie and removed the top three studs from his shirt. She dropped them into his jacket pocket. At the same time she kicked off her silver high heels. She wiggled her toes and bent her knees. "Better?"

"You're stretching my imagination. I now know your feet aren't bare." His hand tracked across the center of her back. He placed her hand on his chest, and his hand on hers. "Ever consider wearing this dress backward?"

"Never."

"Hmmm. I've checked out how that dress was engineered. There are only two hooks between me and bliss," he said, his eyes flaring at the thought.

"You wouldn't," she scolded playfully, squirming as his hand climbed to the jeweled collar. "What happened to slow and easy?"

Grant groaned as her bottom pressed against him. "Slow and easy?" His fingers teased the hooks. "How long did it take to get to the party?"

"Not long enough for what you're contemplating."

He shifted again, pulling her on top of him. The long slit in her gown parted, allowing her bent leg to curve around the outside of his thigh. At first Jessica automatically tugged at the rising fabric to keep it respectable. Grant's husky laugh and his hand that was audaciously flirting with the back of her thigh told her how ridiculous she was being. His knee nudged hers apart.

"Grant!"

"Hmmm?" His eyes widened in boyish innocence as his hand kneaded the rounded flesh of her derriere.

"I thought only women could be teases," she said, giving up any pretense of modesty.

"This is my special brand of refined torture. Only problem is, I don't know who's torturing whom." Through her nylons he searched for a panty line. There was none. His fingers tugged at the elasticized band low on her hips. He held his breath, waiting for her to tell him to stop.

Jessica raised her hips a fraction of an inch. Now or later—it made little difference to her.

He peeled off her hosiery. The thought of her completely naked under the shimmering fabric sent a shaft of desire throbbing through him. His hand clenched the sheer nothingnesses he'd removed. He balled them, then tucked them into his trouser pocket. "Tonight I kept watching you, wondering about your saucy reply to the question I asked when we left the house. My imagination had a field day."

Slowly his hard thigh moved against her. He felt her heat through his trousers. He didn't know which of them would incinerate first.

"We're almost there," Jessica said. She felt the car swerve as it left the paved highway for the road leading to her house.

"Don't I know it." Grant struggled for control. "You'd better drop two or three bags of ice into the spa."

Jessica kissed him once, hard. Then she straightened and covered her bare leg as she slipped into the far corner of the car. Her eyes devoured him as he tucked his shirttail into his pants. "I'm all out of ice," she murmured loud enough for him to hear. "You melted it last week."

The car stopped. They sat grinning at each other.

"Thanks," Grant said to the driver, who'd opened the door for them. Concentrating on keeping the silly grin off his face, he handed the driver a handsome tip, then helped Jessica from the car.

"Do you think he knows?" she asked, glancing over her shoulder at the twin red taillights. She held her purse and shoes in one hand and Grant's hand in the other. A bubble of laughter, close to a girlish giggle, pealed through her lips.

"He's probably got a tape recorder in the rear speaker," Grant teased. "I'll have to make my first blackmail payment next week."

Jessica scampered in front of him, running lightly up the steps. "Who'd he threaten to send it to? Your wife? Your other girl friend?" She laughed again, teasing. "If he sent them to Rose, she'd make the payment."

"She'd pay double if he planted one in the spa." Grant paused at the bottom of the steps. She hiked up her gown to keep it from trailing in the dust. Several rows of fabric cupped her hips as they swayed in front of his eyes. "I'd pay triple. Something for the posterior —I mean posterity."

"Dirty ol' Yankee," she retorted, waltzing into the hallway. She crooked a finger in his direction. "Come into my spa, and I'll clean up your act."

Grant took the steps two at a time. "Sounds like an offer with an unlimited guarantee."

With one finger, she popped the row of studs from his shirt. "That depends on whether or not my wish comes true."

He shook his head with mock sorrow. "I don't think even the Shooting Star Fairy could finish a pool in thirty days. But I don't blame you for wishing big." The amused lilt left his voice. "My wish bordered on the impossible, too."

Jessica put her finger over his lips to hush him. "Telling someone your wish is like blowing it in the wind. It'll never come true."

"What if I'm certain it's going to come true in the very near future?" He turned her around as he shrugged off his jacket and shirt. "The very, very near future," he whispered, parting her hair, lifting it over her shoulders. As the hooks unfastened, the weight of the gown carried it to the floor. "Soon."

CHAPTER TEN

The light kiss Grant bestowed on the small imprint left by the hooks sent shivers across her shoulders. Beneath the weight of her hair, she felt her nipples tauten. They ached for his touch.

She heard the change in Grant's trouser pocket jangle as he removed the final barrier between them. Smiling lazily, she realized he'd protected her modesty by keeping his back turned as she undressed. Although he knew she'd been married and wasn't a shy virgin, he treated her with utmost gentleness.

"Right time, right place?" she heard him ask, his voice strained.

Eyelids heavy, head tossed back, she leaned against him. "Ummm-hmmm," she hummed against his lips as they closed over hers. *And the right man.*

"The spa is through the double door off the living room," she said, turning in his arms.

Side by side, hips brushing, fingers laced together, they walked through the room without seeing anything but each other. On her way through the door, Jessica flipped two switches. One lit the light in the spa, and the other started the water churning.

Grant stepped into the bubbling water first. He lifted Jessica, letting her feel the heated length of his body, and gave her a chance to adjust to his hardness and the coolness of the water.

Thigh deep and knowing the depth, Jessica had just enough sense left to warn, "There's one more steep step."

Before he took the final step, he removed the combs from her hair. He wrapped her hair around his hand several times, raised it to the crown of her head, and inserted the magnolia-covered combs to keep it in place.

"Thank you." She loved how he thought of every detail.

"My pleasure."

His hands returned to her waist. He held her tightly and made the final step. Currents of water jetted around her shoulders and his chest.

"Heavenly," he groaned, meaning the celestial woman in his arms more than the silky water.

For long moments they held tightly to each other, their hearts thudding louder than the water intimately circulating around them. Contentment and anticipation, peacefulness and anxiety blended together in a heady mixture.

Grant's legs buckled, and he eased himself onto the wide ledge. Her arms stole around his shoulders. Air bubbles surged around them, but Jessica was breathless. Relaxed, she bobbed against him weightlessly.

His hand cupped her breast. Soft as the tiny bubbles, his thumb rubbed against the tip. With a velvet rasp, his tongue dried the beads of water from her lips, her cheeks. Their legs tangled; hers sleek, his muscular.

With no cares, no worries, no inhibitions, Jessica

untangled her legs and slowly circled them around his hips. Her buttocks clenched as they settled high on his thighs. Finally, at long last, she felt his hardness spearing the water between them, and she sighed.

Her sigh echoed the long hissing sound coming from between his lips. She felt his hands trail from her knees, up the outside of her thighs, pressing her closer, then retreating only to follow the same path.

Moonlight spilled over his face. She captured its whiteness by tracing the highlight with miniature kisses. She loved each plane, each hollow, each breath of warm air coming from between Grant's open lips.

His eyes were open, gathering the scant light into their dark, smoldering centers. Jessica rose to her knees, then slowly sank down as their eyes met, locked, and silently spoke volumes.

They were one when Grant whispered, "My wish came true."

His mouth met hers with untold sweetness. Sensation replaced sense. Jessica couldn't stop to wonder whether he meant that he'd wished they'd make love, or if his wish had been the same as hers—to be loved.

He filled her, moving deeply within her mouth. The sharp thrusts of his hips matched the heated thrusts of his tongue. The water made her float and sink at the command of his powerful hands.

She'd always known that loving could be like this. Some people called it decadent, but she knew that the sensuality of the stars twinkling overhead, the smell of fresh air and Grant's skin, and the endlessness of the water surging around them, increased her awareness of how much she loved the man she intimately sheathed.

Nothing could be better. Nothing could be more right.

Her kisses became frantic as the coiled knot inside her snapped. Her eyes squeezed shut. The stars exploded into vibrant colors behind her eyelids. Swirling bits and pieces spun dizzily, orbiting into the deep recesses of her mind where precious memories are stored.

As Grant surged with long, bold thrusts, honestly seeking to follow the path she led to the stars, she clung to him. In one exquisite moment, she knew that he had joined her.

"I love you," she whispered, bestowing her secret wish upon him, knowing it would be lost in the sound of the gurgling water, "I love you."

Minutes later, they drifted apart. Grant's arm around her waist guided her to the ledge beside him.

A smile played on his lips. Although he hadn't heard her whisper, he knew his wish had come true. Since she was a lady to the core, he knew she wouldn't make love with him without loving him. She was his lady, his woman.

"Where are you going?" he asked as she twisted lithely from his loose hold.

"You'll see." With one quick bound she was out of the water. "Stay there."

"Utterly enchanting," he commented softly as he watched her, graceful and nymphlike, scamper into the house. His hand raked across his chest to relieve the thickening blood pumping through his heart. How could he feel completely satisfied and yet still hungry for her? Any doubts he had about her being free to love him had vanished as silently as the night's breeze.

He went inside to look for Jessica, but instead of finding her, he had a moment to focus on her home. He viewed the surroundings from his experience as a builder of homes. In the kitchen, old-fashioned wooden cabinets painted a pristine white hovered over modern appliances. Like the eclectic blend of old and new in the kitchen, her living room held cherished antiques and pillow-backed sofas. The curious blend soothed rather than jarred his innate sense of space.

Jessica clearly belonged in her home. It was an integral part of her. She, too, mixed her ladylike airs with the spicy dash of a thoroughly modern woman. The combination was mysterious and exciting, as unique and refreshing as the spa he'd just enjoyed.

A few minutes later, she'd turned off the bubbler and returned with two long-stemmed crystal glasses and a bottle of chilled champagne. Two fluffy towels were tucked under her arm.

"I thought this warranted a toast."

Grant took the bottle to open it. "Anything in particular you want to toast?" he teased.

The cork popped. Champagne fizzed over the mouth of the dark green bottle. His eyes were on her as she lowered herself into the spa, and he didn't realize he was spilling her wine until its coldness bubbled over his hand. He filled her glass and handed it to her, then filled his.

"Health?" she suggested.

He counteroffered, "Wealth?"

The rims of the crystal chimed as the two glasses touched.

"And the time to enjoy it," Jessica finished, sipping slowly. She turned, kneeling on the ledge, facing

Grant. Her arms rested on the side of the spa. "I don't know how healthy this stuff is, but I like the way it tickles my nose."

"Not to mention how it makes you feel?"

"Hmmm. Delicious. But you don't get rich drinking it. Ex-pen-sive!"

Grant chuckled. "I think I can afford to keep you in champagne and limousines."

"I don't care to be kept, thank you kindly," she replied. Loved, yes, she thought silently—by you.

"Plantation Pools." Grant shook his head. He wasn't going to be led into a business discussion. "Not tonight, Jessica." He raised his glass high over his head, pointing into the darkness, heavenward. "Money can buy champagne. How much do those cost?"

"Worthless hunks of rock, according to the scientists." It was beyond her to resist teasing him with his own brand of frankness.

"How much for the moon?" Relentlessly, he pursued the idea that the best things in life were free.

"Desert and craters. Poor real estate," she scoffed, grinning.

Grant flicked his thumb and middle finger on the still surface of the water. She laughed, wiping droplets from her face. "The price of the spa was submitted to your office yesterday."

She squealed in mock protest as Grant grabbed her and hauled her onto his lap. "Realist," he chided. "How much is love worth?"

Jessica drained her glass and set it aside while pretending to consider the question thoughtfully. No flip replies would pass over her tongue. Her eyes met his.

"Love's a rare commodity. Priceless. Something we seek but seldom find. It's scary while you're looking, but wonderful when it's found." Remembering that she'd decided that neither of them had been looking for love, and yet, at least on her part, she'd stumbled into it, she asked, "Were you looking for love?"

"No," he said truthfully. "I viewed love and marriage as shackles that would keep me from getting where I wanted to go. I valued my freedom over forming a binding relationship."

She heard him use the past tense and knew she should say something witty, but an inane "Oh" was all she said.

"What about you?"

"I was prodded, pushed, and shoved into love the first time. I'd graduated from a girls' school without any desire to go to college." She shrugged, smiling wryly. "I guess I was pushed into the frying pan and then came the fire. And I got badly burned."

"But you recovered?" Grant raised the bottle, silently asking if she wanted a refill.

Jessica shook her head.

"No wine or no recovery?"

"No wine, thank you. As to the other"—She brushed her lips across his, savoring the hint of champagne on his lips, savoring the love she felt for Grant —"I'm here, aren't I? I wouldn't be with you if I loved someone else."

She raised her hands to frame his face and saw how wrinkled they'd become. "You've been in here longer than I have," she said, showing him her hands. "Are you as shriveled as I am?"

"Not beyond recovery," he replied. He swiftly rose

from the pool, taking her with him. Once he'd set her on her feet, he picked up a towel and began drying her. Pliantly she turned one way, then the other.

"I'd like for you to spend the night," she softly invited after she'd returned the favor by drying him off.

"I accept your kind invitation." He followed, grinning, as she led him into the house, directly into the master bedroom. "Years ago, when transportation was a problem, company stayed for weeks and weeks, didn't they?"

"So I've read."

Grant skated his hand low across her hips. "In case you've forgotten, I have a transportation problem myself." He added, with a wistful tone in his voice. "I may be stranded here for weeks or months."

"Hinting, McDougal? Why is it that when I'm being direct"—she poked her finger into the middle of his chest, which sent him sprawling backward onto the bed—"you're being evasive? To use your favorite words . . . Hell's bells, say what you mean!"

He reached up and tugged at her fingertips until she fell beside him. "I scared you by being blunt."

"You're driving me crazy with your gibberish!"

"I want you crazy. Crazy enough to say what you're thinking."

"Are you going to get crazy with me and reveal every hidden thought buried in your mind?" she hedged. She tweaked his chest hair when he seemed to take forever to answer.

"Do I have to tell you about etching naughty slogans on bathroom walls in grade school?"

"Any hearts and initials?" Jessica said, flashing him a dirty look.

149

"None. I promise."

She playfully slapped his hand when he crossed her heart instead of his own. Flouncing over on her side, she set the alarm clock and pulled the covers up to her ears. "I can be as stubborn as you can, McDougal."

Laughing, Grant bent over her and removed her combs. "Isn't it the man who's supposed to fall asleep first?"

Jessica stifled a giggle by making a snoring sound. But the whistling sound that she had her lips pursed to make as she exhaled died as she peeked over her shoulder. He was doing the most incredibly sexy thing. His eyes were closed. His lips parted smiling. Her hair, woven between his fingers, was sensuously being brushed against him from his shoulder to below his waist.

"I love you," he whispered. "No secrets. No lies. No evasiveness. I love you."

She watched with one eye open as his eyebrow raised, silently questioning her.

"I love you, too."

Sweet phrases of love punctuated their kisses, their touching. They made love with the confidence of knowing they were loved. Afterward, Jessica snuggled close, holding on to Grant, wanting their love to last forever.

She was still just a little bit scared to give her love completely, without reserve. Ridiculous fear, she mouthed. She loved Grant, and she could keep her company and her house, too. They weren't threatened as they had been in the past.

Were they? That was her last thought as she fell asleep.

* * *

Her alarm clock bleeped incessantly. Automatically, she reached over and pressed the snooze button. "Hell's bells," she muttered, groggily certain that a ringing alarm clock had to be the original source for mild curse words. She yawned, stretched, then realized the weight across her waist wasn't from the cross-stitched blanket.

"It's Sunday. Go back to sleep," Grant ordered drowsily, pulling her against the curve of his body.

"You sleep. I have to get up." Rolling over, she gave him a quick peck on his lips. When she started to brace herself, Grant's arm snaked around her, halting the action.

"What's the hurry?"

"A crew costing me double time. We're shooting your mother's pool today."

"Good. Kill it, would you? Put it out of its misery."

His hand held her face against his chest. Her nose twitched as his hair tickled it. "Very funny, McDougal. Let go. I have to get up."

"I've been up half the night." He grinned, opening one eye, then winking. "Whisper something soft and mushy in my ear, and I'll—"

Jessica bit the flat male nipple under her lips. He was yelling "Ouch" as she whispered, "Barnyard manure," into his ear. She jumped off the bed before he could retaliate.

"I'll get you for that," he laughed.

Jessica ran into the bathroom with Grant in hot pursuit.

"No!" she squealed, putting her weight against the

door. Quickly calculating the futility, she jerked it open.

Off balance, his weight propelled him forward and Grant hurled across the room. He caught himself on the bathtub. Before he could turn around, Jessica gave him a resounding slap on the rump.

"Oh, lady, you are asking for it."

He straightened and slowly stalked her until she felt the mirror on the back of the door touching her shoulders. "No, Grant, that was just a crazy impulse! I couldn't resist!"

"Crazy impulse, huh?" His eyes honed in on her laughing eyes, then dropped to the dark rosy tips of her breasts. "I'm having impulses, too."

Jessica crossed her arms over her chest, laughed, and shook her head.

His eyes lowered.

Her hand skimmed her stomach, shielding herself from his eyes. "Really, Grant, I have time for a quick—"

Like a shepard's hook, he caught her neck and pulled her forward. "A quickie it will be, if that's what you want."

He muffled her no, taking advantage of her rounded lips. She nipped the tip of his tongue, but he held his position until he felt her surrender. In seconds, she was flowing over him like warm water.

"Do you need to be there?" he asked, happy with her acquiescence.

Jessica paused, wildly trying to think of a way to be two places at once. "I don't want to go, but I should."

"I could learn to hate that pool," he said, setting her free.

"Learn to hate it? I seem to recall a sonic boom voice bellowing in the night about not having a pool put in her yard," she joked. She turned to the sink, picked up her toothbrush, and gave the faucet handle a twist. In the mirror, she watched his eyes light with amusement. "It's too late to install a spa there."

"I've developed a fondness for spas," he admitted.

"Your mother's still an attractive woman. I'll let her use my spa." She inserted the toothbrush into her mouth and wiggled her eyebrows.

That smart remark earned her a well-placed swipe with his hand. "Men don't think about their mothers—"

"Making love?" she finished for him, garbling the words. "Chauvinist!"

"I think I'll leave you to complete your toilet." The Victorian word left Jessica strangling on the Crest. Between strokes she heard him say, "I'll drive you in and pick up Mother's car."

"End of transportation problem," Jessica spat into the sink. Louder, she said, "Okay. Thanks."

Within an hour, they'd eaten cereal and milk and driven into Charleston. Jessica stepped from the truck and immediately knew something was wrong. The Gunite machine and the small dozer that fed it were in position, but the crew hadn't started.

"Surely they didn't wait for me," she grumbled, stalking into the yard. She drilled her crew foreman with a withering, "What's the delay?"

"The nozzle man didn't show," the foreman answered.

"So?"

He brought the arm he'd held behind his back forward. His gauze-wrapped hand explained why he wasn't operating the nozzle himself. "Sorry. I was sharpening knives for my wife and one slipped."

From behind her she heard Grant say, "Guess that's it for the day."

"Wrong." She pointed to the operator. "Crank it up. I'll man the nozzle myself." Pointing to the foreman, she added, "You string the hose to the shallow end and check the scaffolds in the deep end."

Both men sprang into action.

"Now just a damned minute! You can't handle that nozzle! It'll whip you around like a flea on a water hose," Grant said, bodily blocking her from helping the foreman.

"I have a deadline."

"Screw the deadline. You aren't going to shoot that Gunite yourself. That stuff comes out of the hose at a hundred pounds of pressure per square inch."

Hands on her hips, Jessica bristled. "For your information, this won't be the first pool I've shot. There isn't a phase of this business that I'm not equipped to handle in an emergency. Kindly step aside."

"What are you trying to prove? I told you to forget about the deadline!"

"That equipment is due at another job Tuesday morning." Her chin thrust up stubbornly. "This isn't the only pool I have under contract."

"Dammit, Jessica," Grant ground between tight lips. "You didn't get any more sleep last night than I did. I don't have enough strength left to wrestle that nozzle, and you don't either."

"I'll be the judge of that. This is my company, McDougal. I give the orders here, not you." Her eyes blazed defiance. "Privately owned. Privately operated. For the last time, move."

Grant plowed his fingers through his hair, searching for a quick solution to prevent her from climbing into the pool. He didn't give a damn who owned Plantation Pools, but he did care about her safety. She'd taken the carrot once when she was being mulishly stubborn. Could he bait her again? Given the choice of having her hate him for physically restraining her or making her an offer that would benefit her precious company, he hastily blurted, "How'd you like to be a subsidiary of Northern Contractors of America?"

"See this logo?" She pointed to the emblem on her jumpsuit. "It's mine. It's all I have if everything else in my life goes to pot. You can't order me around, and you can't buy me."

Jessica stomped around him. *There's more than one way to get over a mountain,* she fumed, giving him one last nasty glare.

"We're ready when you are," the foreman shouted.

She jumped into the shallow end and took the nozzle from the foreman's uninjured hand. The man who usually shot the pools was burly enough to hold the nozzle between his arm and his side. Jessica levered it over her shoulder. She used her back, shoulders, and arms, plus gravity to her advantage.

"Can you manage to cut the walls and keep an eye on the hose?" she asked her foreman as she balanced herself to withstand the initial blast of concrete through the hose.

"You bet."

Confident, in her element, she yelled over her shoulder, "Let 'er rip!"

CHAPTER ELEVEN

"Sonofabitch!"

The male shout and a haillike sound on the roof sent Grant rocketing through the kitchen and out the screen door. There was dead silence, except for the steady dripping of Gunite from the trees and the eaves of the house, and a small mewling sound from the depth of the pool.

"Jessica!" Grant darted to the half-finished pool. "Jessica."

Two mounds sprayed gray crawled toward the shallow end. Grant jumped into the ankle-deep concrete, wading toward her. Intent on getting to her, he didn't hear the sucking noise or feel his loafers being left in the gray, oozing mess.

"The hose blocked," Jessica explained, spitting grit from between her lips. "God, it was like holding on to the last car of a roller coaster—from the outside!"

Grant yanked her against him. Using the full strength of his powerful shoulders, he lifted her to the safety of the pool's edge and started toward the huddled form close to the other side.

"I'm okay," the foreman called, rising to his knees. "I ain't never seen nothing like that. The hose bucked, then flipped 'er backwards off the scaffold, then snaked around!" His eyes scanned the yard. Admiration coated his words as thick as the concrete on the branches overhead, and he said, "She rode that hose like a cowgirl on a galdarned mustang. Damndest thing I *ever* seen!"

"How's your hand?" Jessica asked, concern for her foreman primary in her mind.

She slung her gloves to the ground and swiped at the sandy grime beneath her eyes mixing with her salty tears. Pain scourged the underside of her forearm with the burning intensity of a flash fire. Her raggedly shredded shirt sleeve alerted her to what had happened. She'd taken a blast of Gunite at full force, a hundred pounds of pressure per square inch. The sight of the burn and the tiny pebbles impregnated under her skin left her woozy. Her knees buckled. She caved to the ground.

"Jessica!" Grant scrambled up to her side. "Hell's bells, woman, I told you—"

Teeth clenched against the pain, against Grant's admonishment, she spat, "Don't you dare say 'I told you so.' " She shook off his hands, but she couldn't control the tears making gray, shiny tracks down her cheeks. "Don't say it."

From over her shoulder she heard Rose's "Oh dear! Another accident?"

"Get back in the house, Mother! It's dangerous out here!"

"Grant!" Rose ignored his command, answering with one of her own. "Bring her in here."

"Turn the water hose on," Jessica ordered the man beside the fence whose mouth appeared to have come unhinged. "We've got to clean up this mess before the concrete sets."

"Like hell," Grant muttered, "You're finished for the day. Do you hear me?"

"Get out of here, McDougal! I have enough problems without you bossing me around." Cradling her arm against her side, she heaved air into her lungs to distract herself from the thousands of needles that seemed to be prickling her underarm. "Scat!"

"You men"—Grant shouted over his shoulder— "pack it up! You're finished for today."

"Pack up and you're fired," Jessica countercommanded. "You work for Plantation Pools, not Northern."

Grant tried to scoop Jessica into his arms, but her kicking and squirming prevented him. Her unwillingness to let him help ignited his temper. He grabbed her shoulders and gave her a sharp shake.

"You've wrecked the garage and my Porsche, and now you've destroyed the entire backyard. I'm taking you out of here—bodily, if I have to!"

Her arm raked against her side from his punishment. She gasped with pain. His threat and her pain and humiliation sent careless, angry words spewing from her mouth. "You've jinxed this job from the start. You lay one finger on me and I'll have you arrested!"

"You little brat. I ought to leave you here wallowing in your own damned concrete."

Jessica rose to her haunches, then gradually straightened. No broken bones, she silently assessed. Her eyes moved around the yard and settled on the bottom of the pool where Grant's loafers were half submerged.

"Get your shoes out of my concrete. That's a heck of a place to leave them! Now I'll have to reshoot the bottom."

Grant's hands clenched, unclenched, and clenched again in frustration. Sputtering, he scooted his bottom to the edge of the pool and jumped. Eyes darting murderous looks at Jessica, he waded to his shoes, stooped, retrieved them, and then tossed them one at a time into the blades of gray grass.

He followed his original footprints up the shallow end. Twice her size and feeling twice as mean, he leaped to the side and shucked his socks and pants. He stepped out of them and marched into the house. One more word from her, and he'd completely lose control.

A cross between a sigh and a sob passed through Jessica's lips as she watched his retreating back. She bit her lip to keep her chin from wobbling. Everything in her blurred range of vision was dripping gray.

"We could flush the Gunite out of the hose and tap into the fire hydrant out front," her foreman suggested helpfully. "You'd probably have to pay for the water, maybe a fine, but it'd be quicker."

Jessica nodded. One-handed, she reached down and tugged at the limp hose.

"You hurt?" he asked.

"Just a scratch on my arm," she minimized. "Get the keys off the dashboard of my truck. Send the operator to the shop for a carboil of muratic acid and several yard brooms. We'll wash off what we can, then we'll have to scrub down the rest."

"Let me see your arm."

Jessica groaned as the foreman lifted her elbow. Swollen and discolored, it hurt worse when she looked at it.

"You'd better get yourself to the emergency room at the hospital."

Tearing the sleeve, she gave a brittle laugh to prevent herself from sobbing. "I've had worse than this. It won't look so bad once I've washed it off with water. Go on. I'll be okay."

"Ma'am"—the foreman shifted from foot to foot—"I seen one of the concrete men laid up for a month with concrete poisoning. You shouldn't fool around—"

"Shut up." She spoke the words harshly, succinctly. "Get to work."

He shrugged, helpless to argue with the boss. "Yes, ma'am."

By the time the hose was hooked up to the fire hydrant and Jessica had washed off her arm, Grant had made a couple of phone calls and changed into a pair of cutoff jeans. Tight-lipped, he'd gotten a ladder from the garage and climbed to the roof.

Jessica managed to drag two-by-four forms to surround the edge of the pool. The last thing she needed was for the water to cave in the sides of the work she'd finished. Like cleanup workers at a natural disaster, they worked in silence.

Within a half hour, men in work clothes began showing up in the yard. They reported to Grant. He directed them to her foreman, who took charge, telling them what needed to be done. Jessica saw a man with a trowel get into the pool and smooth out the footsteps. Another cut the walls into a near-smooth finish, making it ready for the plasterer.

She couldn't look at Grant. Gratitude battled with despair and anger. She appreciated the help, but his "I told you so" rang in her ears. His men had taken over the cleanup just as if she'd agreed to let Northern take over Plantation Pools.

"No," she muttered, rejecting the idea of losing her identity, her security blanket, "no sale."

This disaster would cost her dearly. With the arrival of each man, who she'd have to pay double-time wages, her heart sank. The profit she'd planned on when she signed the contract was long gone. But because of the possibility of a heavy lawsuit for damages, she couldn't voice an objection.

Plain and simple, she'd screwed up.

The throbbing in her arm had changed to a peculiar numbness. She kept it hugged against her side to jar it as little as possible. Sweat poured from her face, occasionally blinding her, more often dripping from the end of her nose. Stoically, she worked as fast as she could.

Grant viciously scrubbed the side of the house with a long-handled broom. Being relegated to the background had galled him. Nothing short of brute force was going to get Jessica off the job site. He'd chosen the least inflammatory course of action by calling his men. Fumes from the muratic acid burned his nose. Jessica's stubbornness burned his butt!

He surrepticiously glanced in her direction. Shoulders hunched, she appeared to be favoring her right side. She'd hurt herself. Begrudgingly, he admired her determination. At his gut level, he realized he'd be doing the same thing if an accident had happened on one of his jobs. He'd work right alongside his men if it killed him.

Grant lowered the broom, his right arm aching. Sympathetic pains, he thought, fighting the urge to physically overpower Jessica and drag her kicking and screaming to the hospital. She'd hate him, but at least she wouldn't suffer. He shook his head. He couldn't humiliate her or destroy her pride by being heavy-handed.

Grinding his teeth, he dipped the broom into the oversize bucket. She wouldn't admit defeat, and he couldn't force her to surrender. What a hell of a mess, he thought.

"Jessica!"

Wearily she turned to her foreman. "Yes?"

"There's two men out front who say they're Gunite men. Wanna see 'em?"

She dropped the cloth she'd been using to clean concrete from a window. Her eyes flicked over to Grant. He shrugged. Her pain-filled eyes moved to the uncompleted pool. Her bruised muscles protested the quick steps she took around the side of the house.

A man she'd met at the dinner party strode toward her.

"Terry Moore, out of Atlanta," the wiry man said, holding his hand forward. "We met the other night. I heard you had a little problem, so I thought I'd offer a helping hand."

"That's awfully nice of you, but—" His pumping her hand up and down sent pains knifing up the length of her arm.

"I know I'm your competitor on the hotel job, but

you were so damned nice the other night, introducing everybody, making us feel at home, that I had to come over and offer my services. No charge."

His kindness overwhelmed Jessica. A tear escaped from the corner of her eye. She glanced heavenward to stem the flow of tears. "Thanks. I don't think I could climb back onto the scaffold, knowing the pool will leak like a sieve unless a seam is bonded where I stopped shooting."

"A little thing like you was shooting the pool?" His eyes measured her up and down. "You're one heck of a lady, Jessica. The kind that belongs on a pedestal."

She sniffed, glancing from her concrete-coated jumpsuit to her dirty hands to her crusty boots. "My concrete pedestal must not have cured," she answered with wry humor.

Both men chuckled, knowing it took forty-eight hours for concrete to harden. "Son, you get the other men from the truck. I'll see what has to be done." His head turned back toward Jessica. "You'd better get that arm doctored."

Over his shoulder Jessica saw Rose hustling up the driveway as fast as her arthritis would allow. She avoided Rose's fussing by introducing her to Terry. "He's going to finish shooting the pool."

"Did I hear something about you injuring your arm?" Rose asked, after she'd politely responded to Terry. She gently took Jessica by the wrist. Her eyes rounded, then narrowed. "You're going to the hospital, young lady. Now."

Jessica shook her head dismissively. "It looks worse than—"

"Hush your mouth and get into my car." Rose

shook her finger in Jessica's face. "So help me, I'll tear that contract into confetti-size pieces if you give me any lip."

"I think you'd better listen," Terry said, stepping aside at the ferocity in the older woman's tone. "Your foreman can handle the rest of the cleanup while we finish the pool."

Before Jessica fully realized what was happening, she felt herself being nudged toward the garage. She opened her mouth to argue.

"Not one word. Your head is as hard as your hat. Why Grant allowed you to climb up there I'll never know. Neither one of you has the sense God gave a goose." Rose grabbed a sheet from the ragbag inside the garage and spread it over the front seat. "Get in."

Jessica's knees sagged as she crumpled into the front seat. Her arm hurt like the devil—enough to keep Rose's tongue-lashing from having any effect. She sighed, her eyes closing, her ears tuning Rose out. The numbness in her arm must have crept into her head.

The next thing she knew, she was stretched flat on her back in the emergency room with her arm extended on a cart. A bright light glaring on her injury made bile rise in her throat.

"Scream if you want," a doctor said as he wielded the tweezers in his hand. "There's no way to deaden this. Can you make a fist?"

She curled her fingers and bit her tongue to keep from crying out.

"Good. Had a tetanus shot lately?"

"No," she croaked. "No shots. I hate them."

The doctor glanced over his shoulder. "You haven't made a sound while I'm getting this impregnated concrete out of your arm, and yet you're going to gripe about a little bitty shot?" He muttered something about women in general, then continued to pick. Minutes later, he sighed and dropped the tweezers onto the tray. "That's it. By the way, I'm Dr. Mills. I'm going to apply a topical antibiotic and a bandage. You've got a low-grade temperature. The woman you arrived with checked you in for the night."

Jessica rose up on one elbow. "I'm not staying. I've got work to do."

"That's what she said you'd say. Take my advice, for what it's worth. Concrete poisoning is something you won't enjoy having. It'll hospitalize you for two or three weeks." He shrugged. "It's your choice."

"One night or three weeks? Looks like I'll be your overnight guest," she replied, resigned to doing what the doctor recommended. "How's the food here?"

"Lousy. Encourages the patients to get well fast," he teased as he helped her sit up. "I'm curious—what'd you do? Crawl into a concrete mixer?"

Grinning at his easygoing bedside manner, she said, "Wrong end of a Gunite hose."

"This may sting." He swabbed her arm, taking one last close look. "You're the lady pool builder, aren't you?"

"Plantation Pools." She blew on the wound like a child blows on a scraped knee after iodine is applied. "We design. We build. We attend the first pool party," she gasped.

"Brave girl. I couldn't have uttered my name if you were the doctor doing that to me." He carefully applied the bandage. "My wife's been nagging me about having one installed."

Jessica heard footsteps approaching the curtained-off area. Glancing down, she saw Grant's shoes.

"Why don't I give you a call when you're feeling better?" the doctor said, taping the gauze in place.

The white curtain whipped back. A fearsome scowl marred Grant's handsome features. "How is she?" he snapped.

"Visitors aren't allowed back here," the doctor replied. He glanced at his patient's pale face. Contrary to what he saw, he answered, "She'll be fine. She's decided to be the hospital's guest for tonight. Visiting hours are posted in the waiting room."

Guilt-ridden because he hadn't prevented Jessica from being injured, jealous at hearing the man tending her ask her for a date, frustrated by his sense of helplessness, he swished the white cloth divider back into place. He stalked from the cubicle into the room where his mother waited.

"You'd better have your blood pressure checked while you're here," Rose suggested quietly. "You look like you're ready to blow a gasket."

Grant paced back and forth, shooting her a withering glance.

Shooting Dr. Mills a withering glance, Jessica, too, paced back and forth. "I don't need a shot."

"The nurse will be here in a minute. Why don't you sit down?"

"I can't. I hate shots. I remember when I was a kid and they gave shots at school, I crawled under a cafeteria table, surrounded myself with stools, and kept the principal at bay for two hours rather than have a shot."

The doctor laughed. "If that linebacker who just left

166

sees me chasing you around the emergency room, I'll wind up in traction. Have a heart, Jessica."

"It's me that he's ready to throttle." She smiled weakly. "You're safe."

Dr. Mills met the nurse, took the small tray, and lifted the syringe. "Ready?"

"I hate shots," she restated firmly.

"I hate traction, but—"

None too gracefully, Jessica stuck out her arm. "Don't tell me it isn't going to hurt."

He grinned. "Okay. It's going to hurt like hell. That make you feel better?" He swiped her arm with alcohol and administered the shot with practiced ease. "Ouch! Just thought I'd say it for you. Now, since you've been such a good girl, if you'll seat yourself in the wheelchair, I'll give you a free ride up to your bed."

"Okay, Dr. Mills, wheel me to my cell."

"I'll check on you later. Please, don't tear the bedsheets into strips to make your escape," he jeered as he pushed her from the room.

Grant halted in midstep and spun on the ball of his foot when he saw Jessica being wheeled into the corridor. "Anything I can do?"

The pugnacious tilt of her chin belied her sweet reply. "Keep remembering that Chief Wampum's pyramid wasn't built in thirty days, either."

CHAPTER TWELVE

Depressed by the day's events and by the prospect of not completing the pool on schedule, Jessica settled against the starched pillowcase. The gods had cursed this pool from the beginning, when she'd spun that preposterous lie about Chief Wampum. Nothing else could explain the disasters.

Light-headed from the painkiller she'd been given, Jessica's thoughts drifted between fiction and fact. Grant took Richmond; Grant McDougal took over her job. Double-time payroll for his men would be the spoils of war. Although she appreciated the free help from the out-of-town contractor, she knew that Grant would see how efficiently his men worked, and then she wouldn't get the hotel complex job. Not unless she accepted Grant's offer to make Plantation Pools a spoke in the big wheel of Northern Contractors of America. Then where would she be?

Woozily she projected herself into the probable future. The name Plantation Pools would be dropped, along with the logo and slogan. One or two mistakes, and she'd be eased out of her job. Then what would she have? No business, no lover, no nothing.

"Might as well entomb me in Wampum's pyramid,"

she muttered in a slurred voice. "Like the South, I've lost."

Her eyes closed. Tears slipped from the corners. For the moment she was too exhausted to continue fighting. Tomorrow, when she felt better, she'd think about Plantation Pools. A foggy gray cloud as dense as Gunite kept her from hearing the commotion outside her door.

"What do you mean, no visitors?" Grant demanded of the nurse on duty at the nurses' station. He plopped the bouquet of roses onto the counter and pointed to a sign by the elevator.

"Shhh! This is a hospital. Yelling at me isn't going to get you into Ms. Hayes's room. She's resting."

Grant raked his hands through his hair. Jessica's parting shot had indicated her concern over the thirty-day deadline. She'd worry herself sick if he didn't get in there to make certain she understood that he cared more about her health than a damned thirty-day completion date.

"Will you deliver these flowers and a note, please?" Grant asked, extracting a business card from his wallet.

"Certainly. As soon as she awakens," the nurse promised.

The volumes he needed to write couldn't fit on a two-by-three-inch business card. Grant flicked the edge of the pasteboard thoughtfully, then boldly wrote, "Forget about the pool." He glanced up to find the nurse's curious eyes on what he was writing. Giving her a dirty look for being nosy, he skipped writing "love" and just signed his name.

"That should ease her mind enough to keep her in

the hospital if she needs to stay. Don't let her check out of here in the morning unless she's recovered."

Giving Grant a superior smile, the nurse said coolly, "The hospital doesn't dismiss sick patients."

The withering look Grant gave her erased her smug expression. "You don't know Jessica Hayes. She may be small, but she'll pack a mean wallop if you try to keep her here."

"Difficult patients aren't rare, nor are impatient visitors. Now if you'll excuse me, I'll put these flowers in a vase."

Summarily dismissed, Grant shoved his clenched hands into his pockets and strode to the elevator. Worry lines etched his forehead. Jessica wouldn't appreciate him cooling his heels in the waiting room while the crews were working. She'd rather have him at the pool site doing everything possible to get the work completed on schedule.

The elevator bell rang. With one last longing glance down the sterile white hallway, Grant strode into the elevator. He'd have to wait until morning to reassure Jessica that her company was safe in his hands.

Morning came early for Jessica. She woke up at sunrise to the smell of roses and the sound of a cheerful voice.

"How are you feeling this morning?" a nurse in a crisp white uniform asked.

A thermometer was placed in her mouth before Jessica could answer. "When is check-out time?" she mumbled around the obstruction.

"The doctor will be in around nine—"

"Nine!" The glass tube threatened to break as she

clamped her teeth shut on the consonant. She removed it. "I'll be out of here by then."

"Please, keep the oral thermometer in your mouth or you'll have to roll over."

The nurse's sunny smile didn't minimize the implication behind her words. Jessica sealed her lips, but her vivid blue eyes telegraphed the silent message, *You'll have to hogtie me to keep me any longer!*

Appearing completely oblivious to Jessica's hostility, the nurse tested her blood pressure. "It's a bit high," she commented after she'd pumped the bulb several times. She nimbly plucked the thermometer from Jessica's mouth, read it, then shook it several times. "Temperature is above normal, also."

"So's my temper. Get my clothes. I'm getting out of here." Jessica barely had her head off the pillow when she felt restraining hands on her shoulders. Her head spun dizzily as it sank into the pillow. "Let me up, darn it!"

"All in good time. Did you order from the breakfast menu last night?"

"I'm not staying here long enough to eat."

"The night nurse probably ordered the standard two eggs, bacon, toast, milk, and coffee. Sound appetizing?"

"Sounds disgusting," Jessica grumbled. She focused her eyes on the nurse's retreating back and watched her pick up the grimy clothes she'd worn yesterday. "Put them down! Now!"

"You have clean clothes at the desk. I'll bring them when you've eaten breakfast and seen the doctor."

Jessica's lips pressed together in a tight, straight line at the nurse's high-handed manner.

"Why don't you relax?" The nurse gestured toward the roses and crossed to the door. "Those should make you feel better."

Her hands clenched beneath the covers, Jessica felt like screaming something obscene at the woman who was marching out the door with her dirty clothing. Carts laden with food passed by the door. She looked down at her green hospital gown and knew she was too modest to run after the nurse with the back of her gown flapping in the breeze.

In a huff, she smelled one of the fragrant blossoms in an effort to calm herself. Rose had sent roses, she surmised as she took the small card that was tucked into the arrangement.

"Forget about the pool. Grant," she read aloud. She reread the impersonal message. Her voice rose. "He's kicked me off the job!"

He can't do that! My thirty days aren't up! She scrambled off the bed, not caring at all about the back of her gown separating. She'd get to the job site naked if she had to. Grant McDougal wasn't taking over her job! Not without a knock-down-drag-out first!

The phone beside the table rang. Jessica grabbed it. "Hello!"

"You must be feeling better."

Her eyes narrowed as she recognized her tormentor's voice. "No thanks to you. I'll be dressed and on the job site in fifteen minutes."

"Has the doctor given you a clean bill of health?"

"Don't give me any I'm-concerned-about-you routines." Mad as hell, too angry to think clearly, she irrationally accused, "You were probably hiding in the bushes yesterday, standing on the Gunite hose, clogging it! Just like you parked your car where I couldn't see it!"

"What?" Grant bellowed, unable to believe his ears.

"You heard me, you sneaky Yank! You probably planned this underhanded attack to keep me from completing the pool! It won't work! You aren't kicking me off the job when *you* caused the accident!"

"I'm coming over there to talk some sense into your silly head. That's the most preposterous accusation I've ever heard. So help me, Jessica, if you show up at that pool before I get to the hospital, World War III will commence."

Jessica banged the phone down. His threats didn't scare her—much. She chewed on her bottom lip, planning a strategy. *If* she could get her clothes, *if* she could escape, *if* she could be at the pool while Grant made the drive in from Kiawah, he couldn't legally kick her off the job for nonperformance.

Hands on her temples to stop the tilting of the room, she staggered toward the door.

"Going somewhere?" the nurse asked, blocking the exit.

Jessica groaned. "Please, you don't understand. I'm not sick. I hurt my arm a little bit. That's all. The doctor doesn't need to see me."

"Get back in bed before you injure your head by hitting it on the floor." She wrapped her arm around Jessica's waist to help her. "Here's your breakfast. You'll feel—"

"I'm fine, darn it!" She didn't feel fine. The floor kept rolling as if Charleston were having a severe earthquake. She sagged into the bed. "Just a bit dizzy."

"Let me look at your arm." The nurse shook her head when she saw faint red lines tracking up from under the gauze. "You aren't going anywhere."

Overcome by dizziness, Jessica couldn't argue.

Minutes later, Dr. Broyhill, her family physician, arrived. He took the bandage off and shook his head. "How long was it from the time this happened to when you arrived at the emergency room?"

"A few hours. I washed it off immediately, though."

"Hmph! You'd have saved yourself a few days in the hospital if you'd gotten immediate treatment. Those red lines going up your arm indicate blood poisoning."

"I'm checking out of here," Jessica said stubbornly, but her voice was weak.

As he talked, he applied a new bandage. "Fine. You'll be back by noon. The heat and humidity, plus the physical labor, will have you begging to get back into this room." Gently, he strapped the adhesive tape into place. "Remember the time I was giving vaccinations at the school and you barricaded yourself under the table? That's one lesson you should remember. You fought it, but you still had to get the shot. Now you'll have to take your medicine, just like you did back then."

"Give me the medicine. I promise, I'll take it."

"I can't keep you here. You can check out, but you'll be back." He closed his medical bag. It made a harsh snapping sound to emphasize the finality of his prognosis. "Then you'll be staying for two or three weeks instead of a few days."

Jessica groaned. "I can't waste two or three days lying here on my back!"

"Your choice." He patted her hand affectionately.

174

"Three days or three weeks. But if you take your medicine, rest, eat, and give your body a chance to heal, maybe you'll get out of the hospital sooner."

"I'll stay." *Defeated on every front,* she thought.

Dr. Broyhill turned toward the door when he heard squeaky rubber-soled shoes entering the room. "Nurse Williams will take good care of you, won't you?"

Nurse Williams motioned for Dr. Broyhill to join her in the corridor. Although they spoke in low tones, Jessica heard what they were saying.

"Doctor, there's a man at the nurses' station who's being extremely annoying with his demands to see Ms. Hayes. When I told him to come back during visitors' hours, his face turned as red as his hair."

"Don't let McDougal in here!" Jessica shouted. He'd won due to the nonperformance clause, but she wasn't going to be hemmed in here, listening to him gloat. Dr. Broyhill glanced into the room. "Tell McDougal to take his roses and trade them in for a funeral wreath."

Knowing that Jessica sometimes exaggerated, Dr. Broyhill chuckled. "Blood poisoning is seldom terminal."

"I wasn't finished! Tell him to deliver the wreath to Plantation Pools!"

"You heard the lady. McDougal's name is stricken from the visitors' list. Tell the other nurses."

Jessica reached for the phone. "Any objections to my making a few calls?"

"None, provided you can talk and eat your breakfast at the same time."

Jessica made a face at the doctor then she dialed her foreman's home number. After giving him a medical

175

update, she told him what she expected of him in the immediate future.

"McDougal is trying to kick us off the job because of the accident. I want the filtration pumps delivered and installed today. Technically, as long as we're complying with the performance clause by being there every day, he won't be able to stop us. The concrete has to cure for forty-eight hours. By then I'll have the plasterer there along with the tile setter and coping man. I'm counting on you to keep the McDougal pool under construction while I'm stuck in here."

"What if he gets the police to evict us from the premises?"

"That takes a court order. Keep me posted. I'll call Louise about the necessary schedule changes."

"Okay, boss. Hope you get well soon. I'm not a man who likes hiding behind a woman's skirts, but McDougal could make mincemeat out of me. I'd rather face a fire-breathing dragon!"

For the first time all day, Jessica grinned as she imagined McDougal as a fire-breathing sphinx protecting the tomb of Chief Wampum, snorting flames from his nose, and her foreman quivering at the bottom of the pool. "Call me if he causes any problems. 'Bye."

Bound and determined to get well as quickly as possible, Jessica ate her breakfast. But even though she was being what Dr. Broyhill wryly called "a good girl," she ate seven breakfasts before the antibiotics he prescribed finally conquered the poisoning.

During those seven days, Jessica kept in daily contact with her foreman. The McDougal pool was completed, filled, and given its first charge of chemicals.

After the first day, Grant McDougal stopped coming to the hospital. On the third day, after she'd repeatedly hung up on him, he'd quit calling. Each day more flowers arrived. She enjoyed the flowers—after she'd torn the small white cards into minuscule pieces and pitched them into the trash basket.

At night she dreamed about Grant. Thankfully, by morning, she couldn't remember the explicitness of the dreams. Only a hint of starlight, water, and murmured words of love plagued her thoughts. Moonlight and magic. Each morning she berated herself for being so easily duped.

How many times did she have to get hurt before she learned that emotional entanglements and business don't mix?

Like the general he'd been named after, Grant must have planned his strategy carefully. The Northern conglomerate, Grant's army, consisted of carpenters, electricians, plumbers, heating and air-conditioning men, and architects. One small company was missing: a pool builder. From the beginning, he'd wanted Plantation Pools, not the owner. His loud protest about building a pool in his mother's backyard and the romantic skirmishes between them had been decoys to lure her away from seeing that Grant eventually planned to attack and conquer.

Vowing never to be conquered, she concentrated on rebuilding her defenses while her foreman cleared the battlefield by completing the pool. General Grant had won a few battles, but he'd never win the war. Plantation Pools would never be a part of Northern.

Rose visited regularly. Only once did she put her Water-Devil mouth into action. Politely but firmly,

Jessica informed her that mentioning Grant's name would get her on the restricted list, too. After the warning, Rose had hushed. She'd put a hornet's nest under her son's foundation, but knowing Jessica was ill made her restrain herself from stirring up any trouble. Once Jessica was back on her feet, she'd resume her reconstruction efforts on behalf of the star-crossed lovers.

The last night of her hospital confinement, Rose handed her a check for the final payment on the pool. Jessica's throat clogged with emotion when she read Grant's signature on the bottom line. It was like reading an abbreviated version of a surrender treaty. Rose merely smiled, then offered to pick up her the next morning to drive her home.

As Jessica dressed to leave, she wondered if she really had won the final victory. She didn't feel victorious. In fact, she seriously doubted that Plantation Pools was much of a victory prize compared to her losses.

She finished packing her overnight case and strode to the door. Impatient to get home, change into her jumpsuit, and check the work that had been accomplished, she looked down the hallway for Rose. The regulation wheelchair she was required to ride in was beside the door. She heard the elevator bell ring and saw Grant walk out of it.

"Darn you, Rose McDougal," she muttered, knowing she'd been tricked. She could almost feel the intensity of Grant's blue eyes as they swept over her from head to toe. "I'll call a cab," she called in his direction, then hastily turned back into her room.

Her back to the door, she felt a breeze as it was firmly closed.

"Put the phone down," Grant ordered. "I'm taking you." He had several surprises in store for Jessica. A cab driver wasn't one of them. He'd take her—one hell of a lot farther than she planned on going.

"I'll walk first. Ten miles. Uphill." From behind the silky curtain of her hair, she could see him flinch at each word. "Barefoot," she added for good measure.

"Lady, I strongly suggest you put the phone down, or you're going to have to be treated for a bruised bottom before you leave."

As if his icy tone had affected the temperature of the room, Jessica shivered. "You should learn to accept defeat graciously."

"Get your purse. I'm going to count to five, and you'd better be in that chair, ready to go."

"You can't make me." From the sparks shooting in her direction, she knew he could and would. Why make a scene? He might threaten violence, but she knew he wouldn't hurt her. Sarcasm spoiled her polite "Okay, Mr. McDougal. I appreciate your kind offer to take me home."

Grant opened the door and brought in the wheelchair. As she sat down, she wondered whether she should have turned her back on him. He seemed to exude contained anger. Again, she reassured herself that he wouldn't physically hurt her. Maybe a short little fall down an elevator shaft, but nothing that would do any real damage.

He wheeled her down the hall and into the elevator so quickly, she barely had time to wave to the nurses.

179

"The wheelchair races aren't scheduled until Saturday morning," she taunted bravely.

She watched him push the first-floor button without so much as glancing at her. *So far, so good,* she thought with trepidation as she felt his hands rest gently on her shoulders, near her neck.

Inside the small enclosure, she could hear him breathe and smell his aftershave. To touch him, she would merely have to reach over her shoulder. She couldn't allow herself that pleasure. She reminded herself that the silent man was her sworn enemy. She wasn't about to let herself be fooled three times. Once by Nicky should have been enough, but twice by the same man was downright foolhardy!

Grant walked her to his car. "Notice the damage has been repaired."

"There are some things that can't be repaired," she said, tilting her chin up at him meaningfully. She watched his lips flatten against his teeth. His hand rapped against the fender ominously. "Don't dent it again and blame it on me."

Her door slammed more forcefully than necessary. She smiled. Tormenting Grant was making her feel better than her extended stay in the hospital had. Maybe she should have agreed to see him after all. She hadn't felt this alive since— She barred her mind from thinking about the night he'd spent at her house.

"Home, McDougal," she ordered imperiously once he was in the driver's seat. His lips moved silently. *Hell's bells,* she lipread. "Chauffeurs aren't permitted to swear."

Grant started the engine, gunned the motor, and

tossed a thick envelope from the dashboard onto her lap.

"Your check was sufficient. I don't need a lengthy document stating your terms of surrender." She shot him a cheeky, smug smile and put the envelope back on the dashboard. "I'm not among the walking wounded now."

"I'm taking you by Mother's pool," he stated irrevocably. "Buckle up."

"My, my, McDougal. Your 'buckle up' sounded like 'shut up.'"

He shot her a narrowed glance. "Remember the sign on the path beside my house? The one that says 'Don't tease the alligators'?"

"After the huge helping of humble pie you had to eat when the pool was completed, I wouldn't think you'd be hungry," she goaded.

Within minutes Grant had parked his car in exactly the same spot where she'd mashed it. Wordlessly, he climbed from the Porsche, circled the car, and opened her door. Cupping her elbow, he led her to the gate in the six-foot-tall wooden fence that surrounded the pool. She tossed back her long hair and looked up at him. A small, sad smile curved his lips. Instantly she regretted her sniper tactics.

"Grant—"

The gate opened without him touching it.

"Surprise!"

Her mouth gaping, Jessica turned to see all the people who had worked on the pool, plus Rose and Louise, standing there grinning from ear to ear.

"We design. We build. We attend the first pool

party!" Louise said enthusiastically. "For a while we were afraid you weren't going to make it!"

Rose hugged her. "Sorry I couldn't pick you up at the hospital, but I had tons of food to prepare."

Everyone came up and shook her hand or hugged her, congratulating her on the beautiful pool—everyone but the person who counted most, she realized. He crossed to the portable bar and poured himself a glass of champagne. Silently, he raised his glass, then turned his back to her.

Her foreman looped his arm around her shoulders and whispered, "Did you see a copy of the contract he had Kenneth draw up?" He pointed to a tall, dark-haired, slender man wearing glasses, who smiled engagingly at her and waved.

"Contract?" Stunned, Jessica hadn't the slightest idea of what he was talking about.

"The spa contract! Louise says we'll make more off the spas we're going to install at the hotel complex than we would if we built the pool. McDougal said I wasn't to bother you about the details of installing the spa at his house. He said it was time I earned my supervisor's salary. I'm certain that's what cinched the deal. Everything ran like clockwork."

Jessica wanted to break loose from the crowd and rush to Grant's side, but she couldn't. She was the guest of honor. Duty called.

"Did you notice the extras Mr. McDougal added to the contract? I know you thought we lost our Plantation Pools shirt the day of the accident, but we didn't." He walked her to the edge of the pool. "See the rose done in tile? An extra. And the fountain? Another extra. And the special heated spa he had installed for his mother? I'll bet the extras are more than the original contract. I personally hand-carried the check to Louise. She's already deposited it in the bank!"

"That's wonderful," Jessica said, remembering the caustic remarks she'd made between the hospital and the house. She felt small enough to walk under the fence with the gate closed. "Wonderful."

"Where'd you leave the contract? Wait till you see it!"

"On the dashboard of his car."

"You wait right here, and I'll get it for you."

Jessica turned from the pool, staring at Grant's hunched shoulders. She willed him to turn around to see the apology written all over her face. His shoulders straightened, but he didn't turn.

"My dear, come have some brunch before those starving men devour it," Rose called. "You're looking absolutely weak-kneed."

"In a minute," Jessica answered, concentrating on getting Grant to look at her.

Ever so slowly, more slowly than slow motion, Grant turned.

"I'm sorry," she mouthed.

He gave a curt nod and quickly resumed the same position.

That won't do, she silently chastized, striding toward him. To hell with being a belle, a lady, she wasn't going to wait any longer. Duty be damned!

She joined him at the bar. "Grant, could I see you for a moment?"

"I'm not safe right now," he mumbled, looking all around her but never meeting her eyes. He'd accepted her apology. At his gut level, he'd known her barbs were a protective device. She'd fought him the only way a lady could—with her wits. Conversely, what he was contemplating was far from gentlemanly.

Quite bluntly, he wanted to throw her over his shoulder and claim her in a man's most primitive manner. Whether she admitted it or not, she belonged to him. Everything he'd done had been to protect her because he loved her.

Bite your tongue, he silently coached himself. *You'll never know if she's truly yours unless she destroys the barriers she's erected.*

Jessica sensed, regardless of where they were and who they were with, that she'd lose him if she didn't clear the air between them. She'd misjudged him. Her chin rose and her heart clamored in her chest. She wasn't a lily-livered coward—she was made of sterner stuff. "You added a few extras, didn't you?"

"Yes."

"And arranged for the deal at the hotel complex?"

"Yes."

"Honest, direct, straightforward as ever," she commented. Seeing that he was only going to give her single-syllable answers, she said, "Let's see how far your honesty goes, McDougal. You never intended to take over Plantation Pools, did you?"

"Never."

His drink sloshing over his fingers told her she'd just about reached the end of her questioning. She put her hand over his to gain the courage she'd need to ask the most important question: "Do you still love me?"

"Yes." His eyes locked on hers with an intensity that made her feel as if her insides were melting, burn-

184

ing. He added with a hoarse voice, "This isn't the time, or the place."

"Jessica, your face is awfully flushed," her foreman noted as he handed her the thick envelope. "Maybe you'd better get out of the heat and go inside for a few minutes. I'm sure everybody will understand since you came directly from the hospital to the party."

Playing the swooning southern belle for the first time in her life, she leaned heavily against Grant. She fluttered her lashes beguilingly and said in a voice everyone could hear, "I'm feeling faint. Could you carry me into the house?" *Sotto voce,* she added, "And I don't mean drive, I mean carry."

Grant swept her into his arms. "Rose, pack up the party and take it to my house. Jessica is feeling . . . poorly."

As he carried her by his mother, Jessica gave her a happy wink. Rose nodded her approval. After all, there are times when being a belle had certain advantages. Much as Rose wanted to postpone the Reconstruction until she could play a major role, she handed everyone a plate of food and shooed them toward the back gate.

Inside the house, Grant climbed the curved staircase, holding Jessica closely against him.

"Grant, one more question." Half afraid of his answer to the question pounding from her heart to her brain, she burrowed her face against his neck. "Will you marry me?"

His arms tightened. She felt him swallow deeply. But he didn't say anything! Did that mean he hated telling her no? She babbled, "I know this may not be the time or the place, and it's not fitting for a lady to

185

propose to a man, not even with his mother's permission—"

"Yes!" Grant bellowed in the same sonic-boom voice he'd used the night they'd met. Laughter swelled from his chest, spilling over them. "Hell's bells, yes!"

Jessica hugged him, kissed him over and over, squirming in his arms, telling him how much she loved him, wanted him, wanted to be his wife, forever. When she felt him sway, she glanced over her shoulders at the steep stairs. "I guess you'll have to put up with me doing things in the wrong places."

Her redheaded Rhett Butler, with his intense blue eyes, answered as he should have. "Frankly, my dear, I don't give a damn."

JAYNE CASTLE

excites and delights you with
tales of adventure and romance

____TRADING SECRETS

Sabrina had wanted only a casual vacation fling with the
rugged Matt. But the extraordinary pull between them
made that impossible. So did her growing relationship
with his son—and her daring attempt to save the boy's life.
19053-3-15 $3.50

____DOUBLE DEALING

Jayne Castle sweeps you into the corporate world of
multimillion dollar real estate schemes and the very
private world of executive lovers. Mixing business with
pleasure, they made *passion* their bottom line.
12121-3-18 $3.95

ROBERTA GELLIS

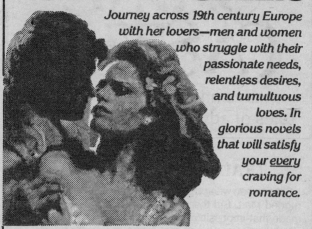

Journey across 19th century Europe with her lovers—men and women who struggle with their passionate needs, relentless desires, and tumultuous loves. In glorious novels that will satisfy your every craving for romance.